I0732097

Mulberry Cove

By Tecla Emerson

Mulberry Cove © 2022 by Tecla Emerson

All rights reserved. No part of this publication may be reproduced, stored in a retrieval system, or transmitted by any means without the written permission of the author. Exception allowed for brief quotations in printed reviews in a magazine, newspaper or the Web.

ISBN: 978-1-7377615-2-5

Edited by P.F. Klyce

Cover Design by PaperinthePark.com

Page Design by Robert Henry
http://RightHandPublishing.com

Printed in the United States of America
Published by OutLook Press
Pub3000@aol.com

"If there is no struggle, there is no progress."
—Frederick Douglass

INTRODUCTION . . .

Mother left when I was sixteen. I had just completed my junior year of high school. That summer, the adults in my life decided it would be best for me to stay with my grandmother. She lived in South Carolina, and I really didn't know her very well.

It was the longest summer of my life! Grandmother, I called her Grandmom, and I both tried to come to grips with what had "happened" to mother. I'm still not sure if we helped each other, or just dragged each other further down. It was a crazy time. I made a habit of taking long walks along the paths and trails that had been cut out of the Carolina lowlands where she lived.

Did I learn anything that summer? Not much that I can remember – except that I'd never adjust to loneliness. In my wanderings, I spent a good deal of time at a dilapidated old house. It was on the plantation adjacent to

Grandmom's home. It was a ways down a path that trailed through an overgrown collection of live oaks. They were huge. I'd never seen the like. They were draped in odd-looking, long grey tendrils. Coming from the North, I'd never heard of Spanish moss – let alone seen it. It hung in wispy ghost-grey twists from nearly every branch of the old trees. It created an ethereal look to the forest when it swayed in the breeze. Grandmom said it had always been part of the landscape. I sort of liked it, although it was spooky.

The ruins that I discovered that summer had once been the property of Grandmom's nearest neighbor. It was now almost totally hidden in an overgrown tangle of weeds and untrimmed bushes. What remained of the buildings suggested that long ago it was all part of a thriving plantation. There was little left. The huge main house now had most of its brick walls still standing. Further down the hill was a skeleton of what had probably been a massive barn. At the bottom of the hill, there were two rows of tumbledown old shacks – ending near a pier that jutted out into a lazy creek that barely moved in the heat of a the summer's day. I walked part of the way out on the pier. and decided that it was probably being held together by cobwebs. And truly, I didn't much care if it collapsed under me. I was just plain worn-out from being so bored. This, however, was where I spent many an afternoon. Sometimes I brought a book with me, sometimes my sketchpad, sometimes my music. But I soon realized that the music interrupted a silence that I had never heard before. An occasional stray bird chirped, but otherwise, the quiet was so intense, it was deafening. Sometimes I would snap my fingers just to hear a sound so that I knew I was still part of this world.

One day toward the middle of summer – when the heat was especially oppressive and I was once again totally bored – I thought I might just walk and never stop. I was paying little attention as my steps took me down the path to the dilapidated old house on the plantation. With little thought, I made my way up sagging wood stairs to an ancient porch where the boards creaked with each step. I carefully opened what must have been a grand front door. The hinges let out a muffled screech. Not sure if I should even be there, I let curiosity get the better of me, and stepped inside. Every corner of what surely had been a grand home held piles of trash and debris. Most of the glass window panes were either cracked or shattered. The few remaining doors were mostly hanging by one hinge, if they were still attached at all. There was hardly any furniture. The floors were very creaky but mostly intact. It was eerie hearing nothing but my footsteps treading through the dirt and dust.

In the kitchen I pushed around the debris, finding little more than some broken cups and dented and rusted pots. There were a few old glass bottles, most were cracked. Then, I spotted an old door with no handle – partly hidden behind a couple of collapsing wooden crates. My curiosity got the better of me! I stuck a finger through the hole where a handle had once been and tried to pull the door open. It creaked. The wood, swollen from years of dampness, really didn't want to give, but a good yank fixed that! Behind the door was the interior of a small closet, not very deep and with only two shelves. But there on the bottom shelf was a dark maroon book. It took only a moment to discover that it was filled with faded writing. Beneath that was what looked like a ledger. It looked as if it had been through a flood. The pages were stuck together and the writing was barely legible. Curiosity and plain old boredom once again got the better of me. I blew the dust off and peeled a couple of pages apart. The words were almost indecipherable, but I tried to read something of what had been recorded. There were lists of dates and numbers of cotton bales sold and the prices fetched for them, which was difficult to decipher in the ancient penmanship. There were words too – many words I'd never known before. But one nearly jumped off the page: *manumission*. Well, I knew what that meant. I hadn't slept through my entire sophomore history class! Then on other pages – lists of purchases and sales – of people! Human beings. Young, old, women, men. I knew about slavery.

Here was something that I could try to make sense of. Maybe put the pieces together of this once upon a time thriving plantation. My dream had always been to write. Back at school, my English teacher had actually said to me that she thought I had a gift when it came to the written word. Well, here was my chance!

Looking at the smeared and almost indecipherable pages of both books, I was sure there was a tale to be told here. Here was a recording of long-ago events – something we only read about in history books – or learned of at one of the dreary visits to historic sites that I had more than enough of.

And so it began – How I spent the last few weeks of my summer away. It took far more time than I thought possible, but by poring through old faded handwritten notes, I was able to piece together what may have happened here – at what must have been a very prosperous plantation. It became a story woven together from the bits and pieces of writing that were left behind. Much of it from a young girl who had kept a sort of diary. There were names that were used often in the notes, like Malachi and Damien. Who were these people? How were they part of this girl's life?

It was an interesting diversion – uncovering a true piece of history. Piecing together all the scratchy, partly deleted, faded notes, I was able to weave a tale together. The tale of a young girl named Amelia. Newly immigrated, she came to life through the notes left behind. And Amelia made a friend. A friend named Dancy. Both may have been 16 like me and from the notes, it appeared that both had been tasked with re-sponsibilities that far exceeded their years.

Abigail Winslow
July, 2022

ONE . . .

It was the lookout who saw them first. The Yanks, that is. I was not supposed to be on deck. In truth, I wasn't. I was balancing on the top step of the ladder that led to our quarters.

The lookout made three quiet taps on the deck. That was the signal announcing that there were three ships in the area. The darkness would keep us hidden. But because sound travels remarkably well over the water, we had been instructed that silence was of the utmost importance if another ship was in our area.

While walking the deck last evening, I asked the captain what would happen if the Yanks caught us running the blockade. His answer was brief, as his dark eyes scanned the horizon.

"Sink us," he answered. "There's a war on."

And here we were. One thing I was sure of, if they were going to sink us, I was going to be on deck and not stuck in that crowded, airless, foul-smelling cabin with the others.

It was very early in the morning before the sun even thought of peeking over the horizon. I couldn't sleep. The only sound I could hear was the swish of water as we cut through the waves. The moonless sky was nearly black, which meant storm clouds were hiding the stars. The air felt damp, foreboding, and almost frightening. The captain said this was what he was hoping for. What? I wondered. I stepped out onto the deck, unable to resist a look at what was taking place.

There was no warning.

A tremendous boom, nearly knocked me off my feet as it crashed through the pitch-black darkness. The explosion lit up the sky. It allowed a brief look at the dark silhouette of a not very far off ship. A ship that was steaming toward us. "Damnation." The captain was at the wheel. "Hard alee," he yelled, no longer using the whisper that kept us hidden. The ship leaned to one side as the direction was abruptly changed. Boards creaked, sails flapped. The sound of feet running across aged boards echoed through the darkness. Another blast. A frightening tremor ran down the length of the ship.

"Damnation," he said again – only this time

much louder and with undisguised anger in his voice.

In the flash of the canon, the blackness of the night lit up. The silhouette that I saw was of a ship. A ship far larger than ours. It was approaching from the side. There was no doubt we would soon be overtaken. We had one small canon and, according to the crew, the range was not great. They laughed when I asked if it would protect us from the Yankees.

"Over to lee," cried a sailor, pointing to some distant point. Barely visible was a puffy cloud-like image hovering over the blackness of the ocean. There was no confusing it. I had lived in England long enough to know a fog bank when I saw one. Another huge boom shook the night! A cannonball crossed our bow – it missed its intended mark, only shattering part of the side rail. The sound of splintering wood was frightening. There was a tremendous splash. The canon ball sank into the briny deep, its damage done.

Within seconds, we slipped into the thick mist. The fog enveloped us like a great grey protective blanket. We disappeared from view. We were silent again as the captain signaled the sailors to come down from the rigging. We slipped along with only the sound of a quiet shush as the bow sliced through the dark water. I suspected our pursuer wouldn't follow us into the fog.

Why was it that no one had felt a need to inform me before I boarded this ship in Southampton that I was booking passage on a blockade-runner! Their country, the United States of America, was at war and there was a very good chance we could be captured or worse! Why was I not informed of this until we were halfway across the Atlantic?

The ship did have a strange look about her, which I determined when I first set eyes on her. She was low and sleek and had a chimney amid ship. I knew little of such things, and remember thinking only that this ship would be going to where I needed to go. How would I have known of such things as blockade-runners and ships firing at each other?

My uncle had written that I was to board the first ship that I could book passage on – one that would be sailing to South Carolina in the United States of America. This had not been so easy. Few ships were taking passengers across the ocean. When I found one that agreed to take me, it nearly depleted the little money that was left in my purse. It had taken more than a month of journeying daily to the waterfront to find a ship that was planning to cross the ocean. And I had been told to accept passage on the first such ship that could be found.

It was my first trip out of Yorkshire, not that far north of London. And it was my first venture alone. "Young ladies," as Sister Teresa had stressed with a scowl, "do not travel unaccompanied!" But there had been no one at the school to accompany me and, as Sister said, girls were often married at my age. So, she said, in her usual stern voice, I was certainly old enough to ride in a coach to Southampton without an escort. I do believe she would have been happier had I chosen to be married. Then she could have washed her hands of me. And, she added, what with the war raging in America, there was no one to accompany me on my overseas travels. I do believe what she really meant was that a lack of funds from my inheritance would preclude anyone from escorting me on my journey.

Then, in an attempt to get me moving along, she gave me the name of a friend. Her friend, she said, owned a boarding house in Southampton. Her instructions were that I was to stay there until such time as I could procure transportation across the ocean.

This was not typical of Sister Teresa; she rarely extended a courtesy to anyone, preferring to have a perpetual scowl on her face and being disagreeable with just about everyone. Very soon I was to discover that her friend, the Widow Kelly, was no longer at the boarding house. She had recently remarried. A Widow O'Malley was now in charge of the residence.

She was not a very pleasant woman. She was as round as she was tall, a bit unusual with the recent starving times in Ireland, from which she had emigrated not so long ago. When asked of her family, her quick and short answer was, "Dead. The lot of 'em." She said no more. Her rounded cheeks and bright eyes betrayed her true personality, as she was inclined towards gruffness and short temper.

My intention hadn't been to stay so long. When my funds were nearly depleted, she said I could serve meals in her dining room and do the cleanup to earn my room and board. I saw it as a generous offer. In truth, the work took far more time than it should have with little financial reward. During the last two weeks of my stay, I not only served meals but also tended to all the cleaning up after. And like a common charwoman, I was charged with making beds and emptying night slops.

The Widow O'Malley was of little help in assisting me on my way and offered no help at all in obtaining passage to the United States. "You want to cross the ocean?" she asked. "Impossible. There's a war on." With that, she harrumphed out of the room. I was left to my own devices. I took a berth on a ship that I had no business being on.

I do believe the Widow wanted me to stay. She had mumbled something about paying me a handsome salary if I'd continue to work for her. I pretended I didn't hear. Much as I would have preferred to remain in my own country, becoming a charwoman for the ill-tempered owner of a busy waterfront boarding house was not what I wanted.

But what could my answer possibly have been? My uncle, who never asked anything of me, had requested that I come to the United States with all due haste. And here I was, on my way – or almost.

I moved to the ship's rail, not caring if the captain saw me. The fog was so thick that looking down, I could barely see the water as we slid along in near silence. The sea was nearly flat, with only a faint shush sound as the bow cut through the water.

"If all goes well, we'll be tied up just north of Charleston in a few hours. Soon after the sun is up." The captain was once again making his way down the length of the ship. "Get the cargo off and the new cargo loaded," his voice was just above a whisper. He had left the wheel to one of the crew and was inching along the side, squinting into the fog. His eyes rarely looked at a person, preferring to watch what was beyond the rail of his ship.

"Nothing to worry over. Know these waters like the back of my hand. Grew up on the water, I did."

He didn't expect an answer but kept on moving along the rail watching and listening, his head cocked to one side, his white beard spread haphazardly over his captain's jacket. His whole body was tense with concentration. It was as if he could see through the fog and had hearing that knew where each wave met the shore. I tried to listen and hear what he heard, but nothing came to me other than the muffled conversations going on below decks.

The ship took a sudden lurch, nearly knocking me to the deck. Reaching out for the rail, I held my footing. The captain dashed to the rear of the boat and yanked the wheel from the hands of the seaman. I heard mumbled curses as he turned the wheel one way and then another. We had come to a very abrupt stop.

"What happened?" I asked, my voice just above a whisper.

"We ran aground," answered a voice at my elbow.

"Goodness, now what?" I asked.

"We wait." And then added, "In silence." It was a sailor, one of the crew, who answered my question. "We're a blockade runner." He shrugged his shoulders as if why didn't I know that? I must have had a questioning look. "We bring in the supplies the South needs," he said, "And take their goods like cotton and tobacco in trade." He then disappeared to his post somewhere at the rear of the ship. Well, now I knew they called the ship a blockade-runner, I was just unclear on what exactly they do. The sailor's explanation did not sound good.

The morning light was seeping through the nighttime darkness and filtering through the lifting fog.

"We're going to have to wait it out," said a quiet voice that I easily recognized.

It was Mr. Billingsley standing at my elbow. As always, he had appeared silently out of nowhere and now stood in his most formal attire. His dove-grey jacket and foulard of snowy white silk seemed out of place on the deck of a ship – a ship that hopefully was about to complete its journey across the Atlantic.

"We're not out of danger yet," he said as his white-gloved hand touched my arm. I moved away, just out of reach, before answering him.

Whenever we had conversed before, I found it uncomfortable sharing information when I was questioned by him. For reasons unknown to me, he had put himself in the role of being my protector, although I certainly didn't want him to be. I had only recently met him on this ship, and he had made a point of speaking to me whenever we met. He had mentioned more than once that it was not only unusual but also unsafe for a young girl to be traveling alone.

Not intending to be rude, I turned and asked, "Indeed, and what are the dangers?" His grey bushy eyebrows cast a shadow over old, puffy eyes that seemed to miss nothing.

"Miss Fitzgibbons . . ." Of course, he knew my name, and he also knew who I was visiting. "We are not only being sought out by the

Yankees, who do not approve of the trade that America's South is doing with the Brits, but we have now run aground. I'm not sure which is worse, running aground or running into some other ship be it friend or foe. A hazard of the fog."

The greyness was still swirling in ghostlike puffs around us. I could see little except that his eyes were taking in all of me in a most immodest way. I pulled my shawl closer and said, "Indeed."

We spent some minutes in silence. I stared into the fog and felt his eyes boring into me. I was tall, but he towered over me. "And now?" I asked.

"I suspect the captain will wait for the incoming tide," he answered. "We may be safe," he continued. "We're on course for a port a bit north of Charleston, and chances are the tide will lift us off whatever shoaling we've run into." His voice wasn't much above a whisper. "The captain knows these waters well, but they had a few winter storms that caused havoc. On occasion, shoals can develop almost overnight." That was his answer, which was meant as further assurance as to our safety. I wasn't so sure but had no one else to question.

I did not want to return below decks to the

cabin that I shared with the other women. It was dank and dark, and the air was fetid, filled with smells of illness. Footsteps came up behind me as three other passengers joined us at the rail. We nodded politely.

Not wanting to engage in further conversation, I set about my usual walk, taking in the entire deck. I had walked from stem to stern so many times, in seas both calm and rough, I hoped this would be the last.

The fog was thinning. The sun was peeking over the horizon. The wind, as calm as it was, seemed refreshing. A seagull squawked from high above the mast, making his presence known. The seas picked up a bit and the rocking motion of the lapping waves returned. The incoming tide did its magic. We were free! There was a great sigh of relief. No one spoke of our being "sitting ducks" had we been discovered by the Union gunboats.

The captain began his pacing from one end of his ship to the other. "We're close," he said as he stood a moment by my side. He peered through his ever-present spyglass. "Now we just wait for the rest of the fog to lift, and we'll pull into port." His mood was almost jovial. A close call no doubt. But we had made it intact.

South Carolina. Was it really to be? I hadn't wanted to come. There were so many memories that I was leaving behind. I had little or no desire to see the United States of America. My home was in England. I was happy there. Everything I knew was there. Perhaps the circumstances I was leaving were not ideal, but given time, I would have worked out a plan of what to do.

My schooling had nearly been over when the letter arrived from my uncle. Of course, I thought something terrible had happened. He had never written before. Only my aunt, his wife, had written and that was only once a year at Christmastime. Her letters were always brief and polite, with an air of self-consciousness about them. Until the last couple of years when the letters stopped!

It could have been the complications of transporting mail during the troubles that raged in the United States. But how was I to know? And now Uncle had, in two sentences, "You must come at once." He wrote that he would be leaving shortly. He made no mention of my aunt.

It all seemed so mysterious. It was the height of their terrible war –"The War Between the States" they called it. It was truly worri-some. And for the hundredth time, I wondered what could he possibly want with me? Bringing me all this way. Why and for what?

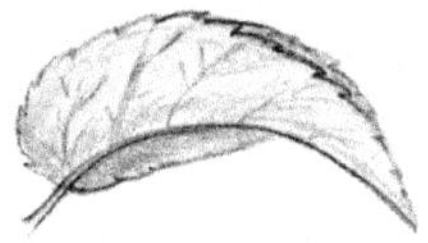

TWO . . .

Aunt Jane, my mum's sister, had left England many years ago when she was just sixteen – close to my age actually. But I had never met her. She had been gone so long.

Very soon after landing in South Carolina, she had married. I knew little of the details, only that it was scandalous that she had left at such a young age. My recollection was that my parents rarely spoke of her. She was my only living relative, so I'd been told. I do not recall ever even meeting her, but from afar she managed the funds that had been left to me by my parents. There was little left that I knew of, but the funds paid for my time at boarding school for more than a decade.

I could not ignore Uncle's call for help, regardless of whether I had received the annual Christmas letter, and was not sure what had happened. I was happy living at school. It was small, and we were all well cared for. Amenities were sparse, but adequate – not at all like the graciousness that I remembered from the home where I was born, but fine enough.

Maybe I could return after assisting my aunt and uncle with whatever they needed. It was hard to imagine what these Americans would require of me, as I knew little about farm life. Perhaps they needed me to tutor someone in Latin or some other subject. Whatever their need, I was answering their summons and I was now here.

"Ah, it's lifting," Mrs. Gillian said. She stood at the rail squinting into the greyish mist. "There now," she said. "I do believe very soon we'll be getting our first glimpse of America's southern states."

"Indeed," I said. "And how do you know this," I asked, searching in the direction that she was pointing.

"Been here more'n once," she said. "I bring in goods to trade. Have a fine business going now, even with this dastardly war going on."

"You are in the trades?" I asked. I knew so little about her and yet she had taken it upon herself to be my guardian.

"That I am. Woven goods mostly. They have the cotton here, but someone has to weave it.

With this never-ending war, they can't get anything to the mills, not up north here in America or to England." She readjusted the shawl that was slipping from her shoulders. "And" she added, "It's getting mighty difficult to find fabrics of any kind."

"You're an American," I said. I knew this but was trying to keep up my part of the conversation.

"Well, of course," she answered, "and blockade runner or not, this was the only way I could book passage. The captain has a load of textiles, many of them mine, as well as other goods that aren't easily found what with this war that's ripping up the land." And she added without even pausing, "You be one of the English, I can tell. That accent says north of London."

"Indeed," I answered, "from a ways outside of London."

"And would you have been involved with the linen trade?" she asked as she wiped at her mouth with the back of her hand.

"Aye and wool. And my father had a mill."

"Did he now. I've been doing this for quite some time, I may have known him," she said. "We should chat." This was not the first time that she had suggested we "chat."

"I know little of his business. It ended when I was quite young." I nodded politely and moved further down the rail. It wasn't the time or place to tell her the story of how I knew almost nothing having to do with my parents or my father's business. I am an orphan. There it was. I said it – not aloud, but in my mind, I formed the words. I'd never seen my father's mills, and no one ever spoke of them.

"Land ho!" cried the lookout, giving me reason to turn my attention elsewhere. No longer concerned about raising his voice and being found by the enemy, he yelled again "Land ho!" One could almost hear the thrill and relief in his voice as his words announced our journey's end.

The sailors scrambled about, each with a certain task, many busy unwinding ropes from the neat piles of coiled line. Commands were given, ropes were thrown; it was both frightening and exciting. We were so close. I felt that I could almost reach out and touch the land. Pelicans were flying low overhead and ducks were squabbling in the water as we slid next to a dock. Skilled hands caught the lines and tied them securely to thick posts.

Few people could be seen moving about, only two young boys who waved in greeting from the shore. It must be a very small town. I knew I should step out of the way, but so much was happening.

Mr. Billingsley was again at my elbow, his hand on my arm. "I will need to leave quickly," he said, his bushy eyebrows only inches from my face. "Here is my card. I am available to you night or day; you need only to drop a line." I pulled my arm away as he pressed his card into my hand.

"Indeed," I said, "I won't be needing your services. But thank you," I added, remembering my manners. He nodded, tipped his hat, and disappeared.

"Don't be too hasty," said Mrs. Gillian, her eyebrows raised in a questioning look. She had reappeared out of nowhere. "He's one very wealthy man." She paused for a moment, unsure of whether to continue but then added, "Not all of it gained in a reputable manner, mind you. Nevertheless, he has more than most."

"That's not of my concern," I answered, not knowing what to do with his card. I pushed it inside my glove.

"And you've made arrangements to get wherever it is you'll be going?" These Americans had no shyness at all about being in other people's business. "You are traveling alone?" she asked.

"I'll be fine," I answered and perhaps with more haste than necessary, removed myself to the cabin. It was a delight to be packing the last of my few things and to be leaving the stench-filled, windowless hovel for good. I would not miss it.

Most had departed when a young sailor, his eyes cast down, mumbled something and hefted my trunk to his shoulder. I followed him down the gangplank where he deposited the trunk. With a quick nod, he turned and returned to the ship.

My feet were uncertain and unsteady after so many days at sea. It felt as though the world was tipping back and forth. My steps were hesitant as I made my way, with care, over to the depot.

A carriage that would be going south of Charleston was waiting for passengers. That was where I was to meet my connection. Uncle had noted, "Get to Beaufort." From there my destination was Mulberry Cove. This leg of the journey would skirt Charleston to avoid any of the troops that could be in the area. Uncle had also noted, "We'll have someone there to watch for your arrival," as there was little knowledge of my travel plans. So much was uncertain with the current circumstances.

A young man went to fetch my trunk and with little effort heaved it up to the top of the wagon. He tied it securely. Holding the door, he said "please," indicating I should enter. The peeling paint and tarnished brass gave the coach a look of neglect. I hesitated for just a moment. The interior was dark and unwelcoming. There were dark images of others already settled in. So, this was my introduction to America. I was hesitant but stepped up into the coach. The shadowy figures may have nodded. The next leg of my journey was going to be a long one I was sure of that.

THREE . . .

How many days had we been rocked and jolted and tossed about in the carriage? Would it ever end? Listening carefully to the other passengers as they discussed our route, I tried to understand where we were and how much longer it would be. There had been a few detours taken that we were told would keep us out of sight of any of the troops moving through the area. While waiting for the carriage to depart, there had been a handful of soldiers who passed by, but we saw no others.

There was little time to observe the surroundings as I had been hustled into the coach. I knew only that we were near Charleston, but knew little beyond that. It felt as if I'd traded one swaying and unsteady home for another, as the coach jolted and rocked. It truly was not unlike the recent Atlantic crossing.

The other passengers had graciously made space for me. We shared greetings with a nod only. Much of what they chatted about was lost, as their accents were heavy and often beyond my understanding. The little that I could understand was taken up with conversation about their Civil War. Each spoke of a brother or uncle or close friend who was off fighting.

The two spinsterish women sitting together had suffered the loss of someone close to them in recent months. Their voices were often just above a whisper, and one or the other would wipe at a tear now and again. They could have been sisters. Similar in appearance, both had sad dark eyes and wispy, grayish hair that poked out from under faded bonnets.

Sharing the hard leather bench with me was a gentleman with nearly snow-white hair. It betrayed his real age. His face was young and without wrinkles. His beard was a light brown with streaks of white. He was blind. The two ladies made quite a fuss over him, competing for his attention. He tried to ignore both without appearing to be rude. Dark glasses hid his eyes. When he dozed off, one of the two ladies whispered that he had lost his sight at one of the battles in the state of Virginia.

The two chatted together in low voices for most of the journey, ignoring me for much of the time. Now and again, they would ask a question that really didn't need more than a nod. Little of their discussion, however, made much sense to me, because I knew nothing about the places of which they spoke. They spent a bit of time telling me that they were leaving their homes in North Carolina to be closer to other relatives. Both said more than once that they'd lost too much. It was none of my business to be sure but they chatted on in what must have been America's southern dialect. It was difficult for me to follow, but they were directing their conversation to me.

"We survived the yellow fever epidemic of last year," said one. "Now we live with the constant threat of Yankees invading our town. It is more than a body should have to put up with." She huffed and sniffed and fanned herself with her handkerchief.

"We've lost so many. My uncle, my sister from the fever, and then my sister's only son. He'd just finished his schooling. Killed in Chancellorsville, he was. It's just more than one should have to bear." She dabbed at her eyes with her handkerchief. "My dear mother was the last. That's when I knew I had to leave." Her voice trailed off.

Her friend patted her hand, trying to soothe

her. "Mother did not have the fever but passed on anyway very soon after they declared an end to the epidemic. Doc said someone of her advanced age should not have been running back and forth and working so hard." She dabbed at a tear. "Not my fault, to be sure," she added, and then continued:

"Mother had been caring for our whole family and then preparing soup and helping all of our neighbors. If only she'd taken better care of herself, perhaps she would have survived." Her handkerchief was nearly shredded as she wound it around her fingers and then dabbed her eyes.

"It's going to be all right," said her friend. "We'll make it. We're going to be safe."

The crying woman's sobs subsided, and a look of newfound determination hardened her eyes. "I will reside in the countryside with my cousin's family. We will start fresh." Her friend nodded vigorously in agreement.

"And you, my dear," asked the friend, turning her attention toward me, "Where is it that such a young girl is riding off to at the height of this dreadful war – unaccompanied," she added, disapproval dripping from her last word.

The forwardness of the Americans had begun to make me smile; they seemed to have no compunction at all with butting into the business of others. "I am visiting my aunt and uncle," I replied. "They've requested that I come with all due haste."

"And where might they be located?" she pressed.

I took no offense in her quest for further information. "Mulberry Cove," I answered.

"Oh my," she said. "Is it perhaps that sprawling plantation not too far from Beaufort?" she asked. "I've never been there, but have heard tell of it. Are your relatives the caretakers perhaps, or maybe the overseers?"

My mind was not quick enough to respond with the type of answer that I would have liked. Snobbishness, it occurred to me, probably did not go well with the American personality of brusqueness and lack of restraint. And so, "Neither" I answered, and lifted a corner of the shade to look out, hoping to end this conversation. She sniffed loudly then turned back to her friend to discuss the weather.

The passing scenery was lovely – a panorama of untamed beauty. Tucked here and there were trees that were clotted with small pink and white blossoms. I assumed they were fruit trees. Their fragrance filled the air, nearly overcoming the acrid smell of a burned and blackened building that came into view. I had never seen the like. It could not have been that long ago when a fire had nearly burned it to the ground. A few charred crumbling spikes stuck up in the air, while two blackened chimneys looked fragile as if they were wondering whether or not to collapse.

"What has happened?" I asked. The carriage passed the barely discernable outlines of the charred remains of smaller outbuildings.

"Yankees," sniffed the older of the two ladies, as she reached over and patted the shade closed.

"Good heavens, how and why?" I asked, realizing too late the idiocy of my question.

"You do know that our country is at war," she said, looking at me as though I were the village dunce.

"Indeed." There was no need to say more. I shifted in my seat so that I no longer had to face them. Lifting a side of the shade again, I directed all my attention to what was outside the window. There were no other buildings, only wild greenery closing in around us.

The trip seemed endless. Already we had spent two nights in different taverns along the way. Our first room was comfortably appointed, or so said a Mrs. Pendergast, the tavern keeper's wife, who knew of such things. I wasn't sure if I would refer to three women to a bed with one pillow and a threadbare quilt as "comfortably appointed," but I suppose it was this or sleep on the side of the road.

That first night, I had been pushed to the floor when I had been on the outside edge. On the second night, at a different tavern, I thought to climb in bed first, lie in the middle, and pretend to be asleep. That way I had part of the nearly threadbare quilt for most of the night. The two ladies lying on each side of me were lacking in cleanliness and squirmed through most of the night, but they did keep me warm.

We would soon come to the town of Beaufort so we were told the next morning, where passengers could continue on with other means of transportation. The coach that had brought us this far would be turning back to transport more travelers.

Our route, so they said, had been free of any soldiers. We had diverted from the main road more than once, thus avoiding any confrontations. The ladies thought they had heard distant gunfire. The white-haired gentleman, who was sightless, had winced more than once at a sudden crack.

And so it was mid-morning on the third day when we arrived at our destination. It was little more than a shack at the side of the road. I was so completely worn that I felt I couldn't possibly get into another conveyance. However, I was quite sure I had no choice.

The two ladies nodded a farewell as they climbed into a waiting wagon driven by a young farm boy. There was no acknowledgment between them.

A young woman emerged from the shadows and offered her arm to the blind gentleman. Saying nothing, she allowed her tears to flow freely. She guided him ever so slowly to an open buggy that looked like it'd seen better days. What must be their story I thought. And then, of more concern, What was I to do? The carriage that brought us this far had already departed, its wheels leaving a trail of powdered dust floating in the distance. Was I to be left here alone? And what, I had to question again, was I doing in this strange and inhospitable country?

FOUR . . .

What to do next? I was at a loss. It was a strange country and I was alone. I searched for some sign of someone. And there, tucked a ways back in a small copse of trees, was a lone carriage. Faded and barely discernible letters painted on the side spelled out "Mulberry Cove". It was a bit of a distance away. I approached it with some hesitancy. This had to be the last leg of my journey! My boots made gritty sounds in the packed dirt. A tired old nag hitched to the carriage, gave me no attention as he was busy keeping the flies at bay with his scraggly tail. A young fellow was slumbering in his seat. He swatted at a hungry mosquito.

"Good day," I said, not meaning to startle him. He didn't hear me. "Good day," I said again, a bit louder. He jumped, no doubt embarrassed to be caught dozing. Leaping down from the seat, he pulled off his hat. "Yes'm, Yes'm," he said, bowing repeatedly. "I's here."

"Well, I know that," I said. "I'm Amelia Fitzgibbons. Will you be taking me to Mulberry Cove?"

"Dat I will." He answered. His eyes never met mine but stayed lowered, as he continued to bow.

"It's all right now," I said, trying to get him to stop his bowing. "My things are just over there." He moved quickly, his bare feet scraping along the ground, trying to face me while continuing to bow as he moved backward to retrieve my trunk.

We left almost immediately. I settled into the middle of the faded leather seat behind the young fellow. Since climbing back up into the wagon, he had said nothing. He slapped at the horse with the worn reins and off we went. Young as he was, he was confident in his abilities.

I was sorry that I had seen so little of the country while traveling in the coach. The two ladies who had shared the ride had taken the trip many times before and had no desire to gaze out the windows and so had tried to keep the shades drawn. It was better they said; it kept the dust out. That had allowed me only peeks around the edges. But I had seen some of the destruction of their war – probably what they hoped I wouldn't see.

Now, here I was in an open carriage able to view everything. The weather was a delight with the beginning days of spring. The world was coated in an endless green. I thought England had been a haven of never-ending greenery, but here the trees were so big and so lush with thick undergrowth, it was a treat to see.

As much as I could tell, and I knew little of fauna and flora, there were huge old oaks mixed with pine trees that were far larger than any tree I had seen before. There were a few scattered white blossoms on some of the trees, the names of which I didn't know.

The forest and wild undergrowth and trailing vines formed a protective canopy over the bumpy road. Although fascinated with the landscape, I began to examine the driver. He was most definitely from Africa, his skin being as black as a pot of tar. I had seen my first Negro just after we had landed near Charleston.

Hard to tell his age, but he seemed to me to be somewhere between boyhood and manhood. His shoulders were rounded, and there were terrible slash-type scars over most of his body. He must have had a terrible accident. He seemed comfortable in his driver's seat and spoke often to the old nag, who dragged us along at her own slow pace.

The drive was long – so long that I dozed off for a good part of it. The sun was shooting out its final rays of the day when the carriage made its way up a long and heavily shaded drive. It was impossible to see or even know there was a structure until we were nearly at the front porch. The huge trees kept the house hidden from view. If there hadn't been a path up to the porch staircase, it could easily have been missed.

The occupants must have heard wheels crunching on the stones as we came up the drive, but the house remained dark and silent.

"Dis way," said the boy as he slung my trunk onto his shoulder. The stairs were creaky as we made our way in the near darkness. We were coming up to a broad porch with grand pillars that supported a second-floor porch. It ran the length of the house. I tried not to stare in awe, but it was near the size of one of the grand homes back in England. Made of dull red brick, the house had tall windows and elegant shutters held back by tarnished brass fixtures.

The boy banged the heavy knocker, the

sound so loud it echoed through the night air. How long, I wondered, would they leave us standing here? He went to bang the knocker again. And, as if someone had been standing behind the door all along, it was pulled open. A tall, thin, dark girl stood in the doorway. Hard to tell what she looked like in the fading light, but she seemed to be about my age.

"Dancy, where you been?" the boy asked.

"Waitin' right here for de likes o' you," she answered, her voice filled with sass.

"Miz Jane be in de parlor," she said. I guessed she was addressing me. I stood as if frozen, awkwardly, not sure what I was supposed to do.

"Dis way," she said waving her hand at me.

Obediently I followed, feeling somehow like a child who was being led into the head mistress's office for some offense. I followed close behind, down a dimly lit hall trying not to be overly curious as to my surroundings. The girl rapped at a set of sturdy but worn double doors. Opening one, she indicated that I was to go in. I held my breath as I stepped over the threshold, not sure what to expect. The servant closed the door behind me.

It took a few moments to adjust to the low

light. A thin spinsterish woman sat engulfed in a wing chair, nearly swallowed up by its size. Her hair was thin and streaked with gray and pulled back in a tight no-nonsense bun. I tried to find a resemblance to Mother if indeed this was my aunt, her sister. But there was none.

Warm as the night had been, there was a small fire in the hearth. The light from the flames showed a thin face with disinterested eyes staring at me. Was I to speak first? It felt awkward as she said nothing but continued staring.

"Your servant let me in," I said.

"They perhaps are servants in your country," she said in a voice that was thin and whiney, "but here they are slaves. You may as well get that right straight off."

"I'm sorry," I answered. "You must be Aunt Jane," I said, trying to start on a different note.

"Oh, bother," she said. "Come and sit. You're late." I moved across the room and removed my bonnet. Slipping into the chair across from where she sat, I had a moment to inspect the room. It was worn. That was the only way I could think to describe what I saw, short of thinking to myself that it was just plain shabby. The aged Oriental rug was threadbare in places, showing well-traveled paths. One of the drapes hung at an awkward angle. There were puddles of wax from candles that had dripped unchecked, and the chintz fabric covering her chair had long ago faded to a washed-out and indistinct pattern.

At school, we did not always have the very best furnishings, but they were always kept neat and tidy and clean. The overstuffed chairs always had a starched white embroidered antimacassar on the back and there were fresh lace doilies on the tables. This room had none of that. It had seen better days, and from what I was seeing, those better days were long ago.

"I see that you're looking around and not approving of what you see." I began to answer but was cut off as she held up her hand to stop me. "Times have not been good. We'll leave it at that. How was your journey?"

I had looked forward to telling a sympathetic ear of our encounter with the Yankees as we came into the bay, and then the long arduous journey to arrive here, but realized that she was looking for a simple one-word answer.

"Fine enough," I answered. I was dismissed with a wave of her hand as she picked up the silver bell on her side table. She rang it once, and when there was no response, rang it more deliberately. Shaking her head in disgust, she was about to ring it again when the door opened.

"Yes'm," said the girl called Dancy.

"Show her to her room and have a bowl of soup sent up."

"Yes'm" she answered. The aunt waved her hand as if we were both dismissed. I rose and nodded and said a barely audible "Good evening."

The girl named Dancy led the way. We walked up a grand staircase that wound around in a graceful curve. Saying nothing, I followed her down the hall to the last room on the left. She pushed open the door and set the candle on the table.

"Soup be comin' soon," she said. Her bare feet made no sound as she left, closing the door behind her.

A wave of homesickness nearly brought me to my knees. There was a sinking feeling in the pit of my stomach, and bitter thoughts crowded my mind: What had I done? Why had I come here? Why had I agreed to this without even questioning? This waspish old woman couldn't possibly be my aunt. How could she be my mother's sister? She looked nothing like my mother, at least of what I could remember of her.

She had been tall and slender and graceful and had straw-colored hair just like mine. It was said I looked just like her except for the eyes. Mine were as blue as the sky on a clear spring day – anyway that's how father had described them when I was quite little. How could this woman be part of our family?

Perhaps this aunt had been in this country so long that she had lost all of the proper English she'd been raised with. She had the slow speech of the American South. I walked over and sat on the side of the bed. The tears came and would not be stopped. "Mother," I nearly cried out loud, "why did you ever leave me?"

Was this now to be my life? How could it be? I had been happy at my school. In another year, they would have let me teach. The headmistress, stern as she was, liked me. She had said that my Latin and French were both fine enough that I could begin instructing the younger ones. I didn't want to leave. It was so far from mother and father. I would never get to visit their graves again. I needed to get back home to England. Well, I thought, that's exactly what I'll do.

I would help with anything my aunt and

uncle needed, but then I would go home. Back to England. The land that I loved. The place where I belonged.

A hand knocked on the door as it was opened, not even waiting for an "enter." Dancy set a tray with soup and bread on the side table. I swiped at the tears, embarrassed at being caught weeping.

"Thank you," I said and hiccupped. There was no response as Dancy closed the door behind her. Stretching out on the length of the bed, I sobbed into my pillow, the soup forgotten. I wished so hard that mother would be here, I could almost feel her rubbing my back and singing to me in her quiet voice. I could remember so clearly how she would sing about the angels, as she whispered to me that they watched over us during the night. It had been so comforting when I was quite small and woke with a bad dream. She would be there, in my room, with hands that always smelled of lavender that would rub my back with a soothing motion, waiting patiently until I slept once more.

Now, tonight, here I was in this strange and hostile land, where I didn't want to be. Tiredness crept into my very bones and sleep overtook me. I dreamt that Mother sat on the side of my bed, touching my back, keeping me safe through the night. My tears dried, as I slipped into a deep and troubled sleep.

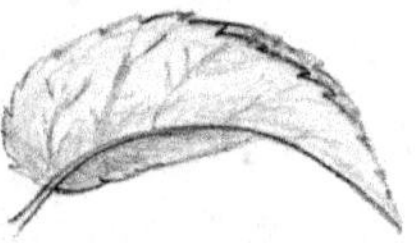

FIVE . . .

Morning came too soon. Everything was hazy as if there was a thick fog enveloping me. For a moment, I couldn't remember where I was. The filtered light peeking through the windows meant it was probably after dawn. The drapes hadn't been closed last evening, and the early light cast long shadows. The sun shining through the windows revealed much of the detail of my surroundings.

The room, large as it was, was in no better repair than the drawing-room where my aunt had received me last evening. The heavy red drapes had faded to a streaky maroon and looked as though they would fall apart in my hands if I were to pull them closed.

The four-poster bed that I'd slept in had, I'm sure, been quite grand once upon a time. The grandness had faded, however, leaving a discolored spread and four posts that hadn't seen a polishing rag in years.

The hearth was marked by bent and warped bricks from fires that had burned too hot and too often. It was now cold and covered by a dusting of ash. The multicolored rug with numerous burn holes lay undisturbed, no doubt hiding more of the broken bricks. A not overly large desk sat against one wall with a leg propped up by a sliver of wood. The chair looked unsafe. Nearby was a stool that had seen better days, a badly scarred table on the side of the bed, and a blanket chest that looked out of place. I wanted to cry. A chiffonier was tucked back in the far corner. It would be more than adequate for the few outfits that I possessed. A few odd chairs, two with faded cushions, were pushed against the wall. My only thought was: How would I ever bring order to this clutter?

It was going to take an effort to try to remain cheery in this new land. But I needed to get ahold of myself and wash and put on something clean. I was in the same outfit that I had worn since leaving the ship. Last evening, I had not even changed into my nightdress.

Growling noises came from my insides as I slipped out of my travel outfit and pulled on my green serge. There were few choices as to what to wear. My wardrobe was slim. My hair was a sight, I'm sure. **So** I quickly brushed and braided it, ignoring that it begged to be washed. That ritual was going to have to wait.

The hall was quiet as I slipped out of my room. The carpeting, worn but serviceable, muffled my footsteps. There was no one about as I made my way down to what I hoped would be the dining room. It was so quiet. I pushed open two great doors. A huge table was before me. Why did I now feel like sitting down and having a good cry all by myself? As I turned to leave, a door slammed at the far end of the room.

"Mornin'." It was Dancy. Her hands were wrapped in her apron and she shifted her weight from one foot to the other.

"Is there something to eat?" I asked.

"Get you somethin' soon's I can," she answered. She never looked at me but stared down at her feet as she turned and went back through the door she had just come through. She was straight and tall and rather pretty with light tan skin and pulled-back hair. Not knowing what was expected of me and faint from hunger, I wandered through the door that she had disappeared through. Maybe there'd be a scone or a biscuit.

Well, of course, it was the kitchen that I

wandered into. It was huge, bigger even than the kitchen back at school. There were many pots and pans piled up in different places, some were stacked on shelves, some hanging from hooks. The coating of dust on them told me they hadn't been used for quite some time. Where, I wondered, was she getting breakfast if she wasn't preparing it in this huge room with no fire lit? I stepped outside through the opened door to find her.

Smoke was rising from the chimney of a small building just a few steps from where I stood. Curiosity getting the better of me, I went to see what this other building was about. The door to it was wide open and just inside stood Dancy, stirring a pot over a fire. I stepped inside without being asked.

"You go wait in the dinin'room. I's comin' shortly."

But I had questions. "Why are you out here?" I asked. "There's a whole kitchen in there."

"Summer kitchen," she answered, and I do think she was shooing me out with a wave of her hand.

Indeed! No doubt this kitchen was separate from the house because of the summer heat of the South, was my only thought. I'd heard bits and pieces of just how oppressive it could get, but wasn't sure if I believed it all.

It was a short path between the summer kitchen and the main house, to which I returned. Wandering about for a bit – up and down the long hallway – I was reluctant to open any of the closed doors, fearing that my aunt might be on the other side of one.

Huge portraits lined the walls of the hall; most were of stern-looking men. Some were in uniform – not any uniform associated with America's current war – but perhaps one from the "big war" they fought in 1775 – the one that gave them their independence from England. And I thought: Look what they did with it! First, they fight us, now they're fighting each other. But I didn't say that out loud.

The largest painting was of a regal-looking gentleman astride a large horse. I imagined that he may have been the original owner of Mulberry Cove. Maybe I would see a portrait of someone who resembled my aunt.

"Over here," said Dancy, interrupting my search for a familiar face. She stood in front of the huge double doors that led into the dining room and swung them open. "Sit," she said, pointing to a place at the side of the table.

I slid into my seat, actually glad that someone was giving me some direction in this big, strange, nearly vacant house. The room was huge and dark, and very quiet. The lower half of the walls were covered in a dull reddish mahogany and painted a muddy green above. A small bowl of rose petal potpourri was on the sideboard. It did little to mask the scent of mold that hung in the room.

The traditional pieces of silver had been set out, most were tarnished. There was a mug of what looked like cider and a stained, but clean, linen napkin.

Dancy placed a steaming plate of some sort of hot porridge in front of me. She said no more but removed herself through the door that led to the big kitchen. I was alone again.

Cautiously tasting whatever it was, I was determined to enjoy it. It wasn't oatmeal, just an odd-looking porridge, and I wondered why there was no tea. Hunger had nearly put a hole in my stomach, and I ate quickly, glad that although what I was eating was unrecognizable, it did quiet the rumbling hunger. Finishing, and not knowing what to do next in this big house all by myself, I wandered out to the porch, where I'd arrived last evening.

The porch was grand, or it had been grand. It swept across the entire front of the house. Sturdy pillars supported the balcony that stretched across the second floor. Dull peeled and chipped paint dusted the wood floor. The brick walls of the main house appeared to be solid, with dull green moss growing in the crevices.

It was difficult to see much beyond the huge trees with their white blossoms that dominated the front yard. As little as I knew of the upkeep of a home, it was easy enough to see that everything needed attention. Walking from one end of the porch to the other and back again, I was careful not to trip on the warped boards. Just what was it that I was supposed to be doing here and why had I been sent for?

Then Dancy appeared. She gave me a start, her bare feet making barely a sound.

"Mistress say come." Not a by-your-leave, or this way, or any of the social niceties that kept us all civil. I was, no doubt, expected to follow her, which I did. This time she led me to a room at the end of the long hall. It was not as large as the drawing-room but still imposing with its high ceilings and wall-to-wall, floor-to-ceiling bookcases. An impressive collection that someday I may be allowed to enjoy. At school, there had never seemed to be enough time to read just for the pleasure of it. There were too many studies to keep up with.

Behind a huge mahogany desk sat my aunt. She couldn't have looked more out of place. Her too-thin figure was nearly swallowed up by the great expanse of desk. Sitting in a huge wing-back leather chair, she looked like a child playing grown-up. Her white mop cap, slightly soiled, was askew. Wisps of muddy brown hair streaked with grey framed her face, making it look thinner and smaller. I looked more closely. I wanted so much to see my mother in her, but she wasn't there. This woman was fidgety and whiny and didn't appear to possess any of the social graces of a properly educated English lady.

She also looked quite ill with dark circles around faded eyes. Her birdlike hands roamed over the desk picking up one paper after another and then letting each one slip through her fingers.

"You sent for me, Aunt Jane?" I asked.

"Heavens. Don't call me that," she said, her voice nasal and high-pitched.

"I'm sorry," I said, trying to think of something to say that wouldn't aggravate her so.

"You may call me Mistress like the rest of them."

"The rest of them?" I asked.

"Yes, you foolish girl, like the slaves call me." Tears welled up in my eyes. It was difficult not to turn to flee to my room or even further, but where would I go?

"Now come over here and sit. I haven't all day." I perched on the edge of a leather chair. As I sat, the fine deep maroon leather cracked beneath me, no doubt from disuse and lack of care.

"Your uncle sent for you," she began, "to assist us with the plantation."

She drew a deep breath, which started a fit of coughing. I rose and poured water from a pitcher, filling the nearby wineglass. There were smudges along the rim from use and from sitting there for some time, but she didn't seem to care. She gulped most of it down and leaned back to rest for a moment. Two dribbles ran down onto the front of her blouse.

"He, of course," she continued, "has left."

"And where has he gone?" I asked, not sure if it was my place to even ask.

"Well, to the War of course." Her washed-out blue eyes focused on me for just a moment, looking at me as though I was the town dunce.

"His hearing, you know."

"What of his hearing?" I asked now, completely perplexed.

"He was deaf in one ear," she said, raising her voice. "He was able to avoid going into the military because of his hearing," and she added in almost a whisper, "and his age. Now, of course, they'll take anyone as long as they're upright." She shook her head in disgust. "They can't win this war. Why do they need to kill off every single man in the entire South to learn that truth." She didn't require an answer but took the last sip of water.

"Now, he sent for you to help out here." She coughed again, this time using her handkerchief. "I have little knowledge of the workings of the land. I'm a town girl," she said. "I don't belong here, and here I am whether it's what I want or not."

"Uncle didn't have help?" I asked.

Again, I was the recipient of a look that could wither the grasses on the Yorkshire moors. "Of course, he had help you silly girl. None of it any good." She began another fit of coughing. "Go," she said, "Leave me be."

I was happy to leave and be away from this disagreeable woman. Could she really be my aunt? She had none of the mannerisms of an English lady and most certainly didn't resemble my mother, or what I could recall of her. It was difficult to remember. She had been gone for well over ten years.

I returned to my room, not sure where else to go. Sitting on the side of the bed for a moment, I took in the too-large room. Was this really to be my home with its scattered and odd collection of cast aside furniture? The room was huge and lacked any warmth.

I stood in front of the mirror for a moment. Was this to be my life? There was no answer. All I saw was a wavy and distorted reflection staring back at me.

Determined to create some sort of comfort out of all the clutter, I started with the faded drapes. It took no time to shake out some of the dust and tie them back. Using the straw broom, I tried to sweep the sprinkling of ash covering the hearth and part of the floor. There was dust everywhere, and it was a relief when Dancy appeared.

"Lunch," she said. Was everyone on this farm this rude and singular with their vocabularies?

This time, my aunt was seated at the head of the table as Dancy brought in platters of food.

Again, I was near starved and did a fair job of finishing the ham, biscuits, gravy, and fresh peas. My aunt merely pushed things around on her plate, preferring to have one glass after another of claret.

A crystal decanter sat near her plate. Her table manners were atrocious by the standards of my school, but how was I to know what was acceptable here in America. The claret seemed to help with her cough. She began to talk and seemed a bit more relaxed.

"I cannot do everything," she started, "much as your uncle thinks that I can." She sipped at her glass. "We've had some problems. If Burke hadn't made an enemy of the last overseer, he'd have been fine." Sip of wine.

"Roland, that was the last overseer, left at the beginning of the war, or escaped, and hasn't been seen or heard from since." Cough. Sip of wine.

"Burke had been rather severe with him, rarely sparing the whip. And after he left, Burke tried to run the entire place." Cough. "For a year he did. 'Course he had his problems, not being one to spare the whip. But then dear Burke, your uncle, was conscripted into the military and had to elevate one of our workers." Sip of wine. Cough.

She swiped at her mouth, not using her napkin. "He promoted Damien to that position. He was raised here. There's a story there with that one, but it's not for me to share." She cleared her throat. "I see little of the man, thankfully, and I must just assume everything is going along smoothly." Cough, cough.

"What needs to be done on this farm?" I asked not sure if I was even allowed to speak.

"My dear young girl, this is not a farm, it is a plantation. Do you know nothing of the South?" Cough. Sip. Cough.

"I know little of this country," I answered. Other than its fight for freedom from my country, but that was in the distant past. I didn't say that aloud. And maybe that battle for independence, so long ago, hadn't been such a grand idea. But I knew it would be rude to add that.

"Well, let me explain this to you. This is a plantation," she said. "We have slaves. We raise cotton. We live in the South and they're fighting a war that cannot be won. We're about to go bankrupt and I haven't a clue how to stop it, and your uncle sent for you for reasons known only to himself." Sip. Sip.

"Tell me of my mother," I said in a voice so

low it may not have been heard. Perhaps we could speak of something other than the trials of wartime America. I just had to know of the connection. "Tell of your time in England and your growing up and what brought you to America."

She waved her hand at me. "I know nothing of your mother. Now leave me, I'm tired." Cough, cough.

I must have gasped. She rang the little silver bell for Dancy. What did she mean? I didn't wait for Dancy, but excused myself and ran up the stairs to my room. Was she so ill that she remembered nothing of either my mother or the country of her birth, or was she just bitter for some reason? Too many questions and there were no answers.

Settling into the rocker by the hearth, I began to write. I had a small journal with me that I brought from school. It was filled with blank pages. This was going to be my new friend. I would record all that happened and count the days until I could return to my home.

SIX . . .

It was only a week after I'd arrived when she died.

I could make no sense of it: How could this happen?

Dancy had knocked with one hand and pushed open the door to my bedroom with the other. My eyes were open, but I really wasn't awake. Lying in my bed staring up at the dusty canopy, thoughts were running through my head: What could I do to get myself back to my own country? Dancy stood over me, at my bedside, shifting from one foot to the other.

"She be dead," she said.

"What?!" I asked, still dazed with sleep. "Who's dead?"

"De Mistress. She dead."

The rest was such a blur.

It wasn't two days before she was in the ground. People kept coming in and out of the house, and I had no idea who they were. Most were clothed in black or shades of grey. One who was light-skinned introduced himself as Damien and said he was the overseer. He may have been the one that took charge of the plantation when uncle left, but I wasn't sure.

Before I had time to understand what had happened, I was standing beside a gaping dark and muddy hole, watching as the slaves lowered the pine box into it. There was a splash as one of the ropes that had been lowering the coffin broke. Eyes turned towards me, but I could do nothing.

All I wanted to do was cry. But if I did, I knew it wouldn't be for my aunt.

The first shovelful of dirt was thrown in. The slaves – if, in fact, that's who they were – one after another walked in front of me and without looking at me, told me they were sorry. One very ancient old man with white sprinkled through his close-cropped hair reached out and touched my hand.

"It get better," he said, "tomorrow be better for sure." When his eyes met mine, I could see a light opaque film covering what had probably been dark brown eyes. It appeared that he was having a hard time focusing when a young boy came up and took his hand. Together they made their way down the rock-strewn path.

The graveyard was the farthest I'd been from the house. There were a number of tombstones there, all with a sprinkling of green moss, many tipped at precarious angles, some leaning so far it was curious just what was holding them up.

Trying to decipher the etched carvings on each tombstone, I could see that they dated back to the early 1700s. Most had the name Chamberlin cut into the stone. These were all Uncle Burke's ancestors; some could well have been among the first settlers of South Carolina.

My mind was spinning. How was I to find Uncle Burke to let him know that we had buried his wife, Aunt Jane? How was I going to get back to England? And what exactly was I supposed to be doing here? And now adding to the drama of what's next, I realized that I was lost somewhere in the wilderness of this estate.

I had paid little attention on the walk to the graveyard and had no idea where we were. The group was already far off in the distance. If I rushed, I could catch up. If I lingered, I'd have no idea how to get back to the house. Trying not to run, I soon caught up to Dancy, who of course had no interest in conversation. I followed close behind her in silence.

What do I do now? I thought as I came into the huge front hall and listened to the echo of my footsteps. Here I am in a strange foreign land, with a huge piece of property that needs attention, a massive house, and who knows how many slaves – all of whom would, no doubt, need food and tending to.

The house felt larger and colder and stranger than ever. My footsteps echoed through the hall. I needed to find an address for Uncle. Somehow, I had to let him know that he was needed here and should return home immediately. Why had the aunt told me nothing? Surely, she'd known that she wasn't well. What was it that they wanted me to do now?

With no thought of what was next, I wandered down the hall to the library, where the big desk was located. Pushing open the door, I stood a moment watching dust particles float through a lone beam of sunshine that somehow had made it through the thick trees that surrounded the house. The room had a silence and expectancy about it that was hard to describe. I entered cautiously, not sure why. The desk dominated the entire end of the room. There were papers scattered across the top, so thick that it looked like an untended pile of trash. This, regardless of my reluctance, would be the place to start.

"Mistress."

I whirled around, startled, not having heard Dancy come up behind me. "Mistress," she said again. Surely, she didn't mean me. The surprise must have shown in my face, but she seemed to take no notice. "Damien here to see you."

"Who is Damien?" I asked, trying to regain my composure as I tossed back my braids.

"He be de overseer." I knew that; I'd just forgotten.

"What does he want?" I asked.

Her eyes opened fully for just a moment to look at me, and she shrugged her shoulders.

"Well, send him in." I looked around the room: Where should I sit? Before I could even make a decision, he was standing in the doorway. He was tall, with a deep tan and dark eyes. It was hard to tell if he was African. His hair was jet black and long and unkempt. His face was clean-shaven, revealing scars. When he entered the room, I heard it before I saw it. One leg ended in a wooden pole or post. I must have looked surprised as my hand clasped my throat.

"Just a peg leg, Ma'am," he said. "Got it at

Bloody Creek. Ended the war for me." I was embarrassed that I'd been caught staring.

"What can I do for you, Mr. Damien?" I asked, regaining my composure.

With a bit of a surprised look, he answered. "Damien works fine for me." His voice was deep, with an angry edge.

"Well, Damien, then what is it that you would like?"

He eyed me with some curiosity, then said, "We'll be needing more seed from town." He paused as if not sure if he should go on, but then continued, "Put in most all that we had already, got more acreage that needs to be planted if we're to have any kind o' crop this year."

"Indeed, and what sort of seed?" I asked, having no idea what in this world he was talking about.

"Why seed for more of the cotton." As he looked at me more closely, I think he was considering the limits of my intelligence.

"Well, and how do you usually acquire the seed that you need?" I asked.

"In the town," he said. "'Course sometimes we was able to save some from the pickin's."

He stood with arms crossed, drumming his fingers, waiting for my response. His eyes were not kind. They were like slash marks beneath thick eyebrows that extended out, keeping part of his eyes in shadow. They were not the eyes of a slave; they were staring at me in a most ungracious and forward manner.

"Do you not have enough that you've saved?"

"Can't save it all. It's tiresome and don't always smell so good and some never sprout."

"Then go and get more."

I'm quite sure he sighed. "We be needin' some hard cash to do that. Cut me off las' time when I had nothin' to make the purchase." He seemed very comfortable drumming his fingers on his folded arms.

"Cash," I said. "And how much do you need?"

"Oh, a few dollars should get us started." He shuffled his feet, or foot, letting his peg leg scrape against the floor. "'Course coins have more value now."

A few dollars, a few coins, I thought. He may as well ask for a hundred gold pieces. I had no idea where the money came from to run this farm or plantation or whatever it was.

"Well, come and see me later," I answered.

"Fine then." He turned to go, but not before

he gave me a look that was far too familiar from one in someone's employment. A flush rose up, heating my neck and cheeks. Was everyone in America this rude and short with their answers? And so bold? Ignoring his attention, I walked with what I hoped was a firm step to the desk. That's where I'd start.

His sigh was audible as he closed the door behind him. His uneven steps echoed through the hall.

Trying to get comfortable in the oversized chair, I picked up the first paper that I saw. It was not a good place to begin. It was a notice from a bank in the town of Beaufort. The letter was to inform Uncle Burke that the mortgage was due, that they hadn't heard from him in two months, and that if some arrangements weren't made within 60 days, the property would be taken by the bank.

Where was Uncle Burke? Did he know this? By my calculations, he had left for the army, not more than a few months ago. I had to find him. But how?! I opened drawer after drawer in the huge desk, but they were all stuffed with more random papers. There was no order to anything.

The more I waded through the clutter, the stronger and the more desperate my thoughts became: I wanted to leave – to return to my school, to be back where everything was safe and familiar and orderly. Back to England, that's where I wanted to go. I put my head down on the desk on top of the muddle of papers thinking only of how much I wanted to get away from this hateful place. As I squeezed my eyes shut, hoping it would all go away, Mother's words from long ago floated through the air – words I could not remember exactly, but they were something like "Life will never be what you expected. There are surprises around every corner." Did she mean good surprises – or the kind that I kept running into since arriving here? I wondered.

As I tried to remember her words, it felt as if she were here, rubbing my back. It was so real; I sat up and looked to see if anyone was with me. Another sunbeam was now streaming through the window, joining the first as the dust particles danced through them. That's how I wanted to spend my days. I wanted to lie in bed and watch the dust dancing in the sunbeams and pretend I was back at school where other people solved the problems. Oh, to be cared for and have others worry about decisions and let me just go about my studies. I tossed my braids back and wiped at one lone tear. Then I promised myself that somehow, I will get started. I will get through this, and then I will find a way to return to my home.

It was noon and I had sorted almost all the papers into stacks, each placed on a corner of the desk, with some piles on the floor. This was how it was going to be. Each stack or pile contained papers related to a single issue. In one corner there were letters from the bank, another had those concerning cotton, one had only handwritten correspondence and another was a pile of assorted papers that I had no idea what they pertained to. At the bottom of one of the drawers, I found a huge ledger book with faded green pages. I didn't even want to open it. After whatever Dancy had for our noon meal, I would start trying to make more detailed sense of each pile.

When Dancy slipped into the library to announce "food be ready" I asked her to bring it to me as I was too busy working. She raised one thin eyebrow but said nothing. Clearly, I thought, this girl does not like me, and sometime, if I stayed long enough, I would like to know why. She, after all, looks about my age. We should be friends.

By mid-afternoon, I had concluded that

none of these papers had been dealt with for weeks, maybe months! Since about the time my Aunt and Uncle had sent for me. Why had it all been so neglected?

Dancy appeared before me. "Someone here for you," she said as she shifted from one foot to the other, her eyes downcast looking at her feet.

"Well, who? Pray tell." I asked.

"Some darky." She answered.

"Well, which one?" I asked, but expected little, having decided that trying to get answers out of this girl was like pulling teeth. I rose and followed her down the front hall.

"Out there," she said as she pulled open the door. I made a note to myself to get those rusty door hinges greased, as the sound grated like sharp pins down my back whenever the door was opened.

Stepping outside, onto the porch, I regretted missing most of this beautiful day. It made me homesick. Back at school, I would have been out walking over the moors on a day like this. Taking a few deep breaths of the cool spring air, I hadn't noticed a person standing to one side. But then, a shiny black furball bounced over to me and sniffed at the hem of my dress.

"Well now, and who might you be?" I asked

while bending down to meet him.

"His name be Freedom," answered a dark-skinned man. He stood with his hat curled in his hand.

"And why would that be?" I asked.

"Oh, just somethin' I's thinkin' on."

"Well, he certainly is friendly."

"He be for you. Keep you company with the Mistress gone and all."

I stooped down for a better look. Freedom was nearly past puppy stage and was very handsome, with a straight black coat, looking something like one of the long-haired setters from back home. His eyes were liquid and kind, but frisky, and his mouth seemed to turn up in a smile.

"Oh, I need you," I whispered, scratching at the top of his head. "Well now, where did you find him?"

"He be swimmin' in the creek some days ago. Yippin' his fool head off." With this, he smiled. "Nearly drowned by the time I pull him out."

"He's wonderful and I thank you. Tell me your name." I said, giving him my full attention.

"Name's Malachi," he said as his eyes tried to focus. They were clouded by a white film that must have made it hard for him to see. He was stooped and wrinkled, and yet there was a sprightliness about him. I remembered I had seen him at my aunt's gravesite.

"Well, Malachi, do you know this plantation well?" I asked, before even thinking of what I was asking.

"That I do. I's born here," he answered. A laugh started to bubble up, "That was some time ago, I tell you." He chuckled, showing a row of strong white teeth that somehow belied his age. "My gran'pap help build this house," he said. "He be the one to fire up the kiln for them bricks."

I turned to admire the row upon row of bricks that made up the house. I had hardly paid any attention before. "How old is the house?" I asked as it was most certainly showing signs of aging.

"Oh, now can't tell you the age, but the massa's gran'pap got his beginnings in a small log shed down by the river 'til they all get 'nuf bricks made to build a gran' house."

"They made the bricks?" I asked.

"Surely did. Took some doing, but after a year or two, they was close to bein' done. I 'spect it took a passel of hard work to build somethin' this size. The old massa' was gettin' mighty sick of living down by the river. Wanted a house up on the hill."

"That's very impressive," I said, having no idea in this world how someone could make bricks.

"Do you still make them here?" I asked.

"No need to no more. We got the buildings we needs and can't spare the help tho' they all got time come winter. This here place has more'n enuf' to do awready."

"Well then, if you know all about this plantation, would you be kind enough to show me around?" I asked.

"Be my pleasure Mistress," he answered. There was that word again! I was not the Mistress of anything, but I didn't want to correct him.

"Fine then. Would tomorrow morning be convenient?"

"That be fine," he said and turned to make his way off the porch. His step was firm but slowed by caution.

What was I thinking? I was quite sure he could not see well. How could someone with not very clear vision show me what I had to see? That, however, I would worry about tomorrow. For today, come what may, I was going to try to get through at least one of the piles of papers stacked on the desk. And now, most importantly, I had a new friend who was vigorously wagging his tail and happy to stay at my side.

SEVEN . . .

By day's end, I wanted nothing more than to go for a very long walk. I had spent far more time than I thought possible at the desk. I looked down at my companion. Freedom had curled up next to my rickety chair; he looked up now and again to be sure I was still there. I had a new best friend. It felt so good.

Tired and stiff, I headed to the porch with my furry friend plodding along behind. And there was Dancy. She was busy hauling bucket after bucket of water, filling an old dented tub. Much of what she poured sloshed onto the warped boards. No doubt she was doing this as she was most likely not happy with a scraggly dog tracking through her clean house. Freedom was trembling as I scooped him up. He looked trusting as he stood in the bubbles that went all the way up to the top of his neck. Dancy, having little affection for anything with four legs, quietly disappeared back into the house.

The sun was setting as we finished rinsing away a lifetime of grime. Together we went in to dinner. He, sparkling clean, although still a bit damp. I was glad for the company and fed him bits and pieces of what was some sort of meat pie that Dancy had prepared. He wiggled and yipped now and again, begging for more.

It had been a long day. We retired to my room. It was such a treat having a new companion. My room no longer felt so cold and lonely. Crying for more attention, I lifted him up onto my bed. I'm not sure who was happier as he curled up in the middle of the goose-down comforter. The escaping feathers drifted through the air, settling in quiet and peaceful disarray.

Morning came all too soon but there, as promised, was the man named Malachi with the wagon. We had finished with our breakfast and were ready to go. Freedom curled up in a pile of hay in the back. He soon tired of being transported and jumped down to walk alongside. He missed nothing with his alert eyes and keen sense of smell. It was a nice feeling to have him looking up, checking to be sure I was still there.

Malachi had started talking almost immediately and had so much to say. I had a difficult time slipping in questions and had to pay close attention to his almost garbled speech. It was a dialect of the South and definitely not the King's English that I had so painstakingly been taught.

"Malachi," I said, in an attempt at a bit of conversation. "Your name, was it perhaps your father's?"

This created a laugh that even made his eyes smile. "No, Ma'am. 'Tis a name they give me down in Shantytown. Don't remember much of it. No one tell me why but it's in the book as Malachi."

"And what book would that be?" I asked, having no idea what he was talking about.

"Well 'dat big green ledger book the Massa keeps. Lists all them names. Names of all the folks he owns."

He owns? I wanted to blurt out but felt I'd shown enough of my ignorance for one day. And besides, I knew about slavery, but here I was, just still not sure if I believed it.But he continued. "Won't always be dis way," he said, his voice low, perhaps only meant for himself. "There be a war they's fightin'. Maybe dis war change some things."

I wasn't sure how to continue but knew I wanted very much to be a friend of this man who knew so much – probably more than anyone else on this plantation.

"Then Malachi is your real name," I said.

"Surely is."

"Malachi. Hmmm. Think he was a prophet. Actually a messenger," I said, not really meaning to be heard. We'd had a bit of Bible study at school, and I remembered some of it.

But Malachi had heard my musings and seemed amused. He flicked the reins on the old mule, and said, "G'wan."

I had so many other questions, but thought maybe I'd start with something that perhaps I could understand more easily – like the trees! Those surrounding the house had thick leathery leaves; they were huge and kept much of the house in a deep shade. Many had fragrant white blossoms tucked in amongst the dark shadows of the greenery.

"They be magnolia," he said. "Neeeeeever lose the leaves. Always green." I don't think I believed him but was sure it was going to be something to behold during the days of early darkness when winter set in.

"How big is this farm?" I asked.

"Down here in So' Carolina, they calls this a plaaaaaantation!" Some words Malachi just loved to stretch out. I needed to remember that.

He had so much to say, and I wondered how much I would retain.

"Got yer'self 'bout ten field slaves here, most of 'em young'uns and two up to the house. 'Course only one still there, but then there be a couple of babes but theys not up to much yet."

There were many questions I had about slavery, but perhaps this wasn't the person or the time to be asking. Instead, I started with who were the two house slaves, but he knew it was coming and held up his hand.

"One be Dancy, the other be Henry. He bad, real bad. He go with Mr. Burke when he git his self off to join up with the army." He cleared his throat. "That be a good thing." Then added, maybe so I wouldn't hear, "Haven't heard tell of him since."

Why would a house slave go with a soldier I wanted to ask, but Malachi was already on to the next subject. I stopped him. I needed to know. "Is it true about slaves being beaten and sold and separated from families?"

He paused. His eyes scoured the landscape. "More'n a few been beaten close to dyin'." He slapped the mule. "Git on," he said. "Massa Burke's wife, one that passed on just now. She 'da worst." With that, he was done with the subject.

Without a pause, he said, "Now over dere's the barn. You can see well enough. Still got us a couple old cows, a couple **a** goats, and a couple a ho'ses, then way down in da' back, a few of them hogs. Git ourselves cheese and bacon. It's all here. Big house use some. Most for slaves."

"An' you can see for yo'self some of the fields planted awready. See that flush o' green? That be the cotton jus' sproutin' up."

I could see it. I wondered how he could see it through his old, clouded eyes. "Them slaves planted 'dat jus' a few weeks ago. Needs to plant more."

How long did all this take? But he wasn't finished. I eyed my cotton dress with new eyes. I'd never given much thought to the where or how clothing was made, knowing only that when one's dress became too short or too tight, it was handed down to one of the younger girls at school. Then one from one of the older girls who had outgrown it would appear. It was hard to imagine the process of how green plants became starched dresses, but for now, I thought, I'll just listen.

Against my will, I found myself fascinated enough to want to learn more. Here was where it began. But how to get it from plants to cloth?

Did I dare ask or would I be showing how much practical knowledge I lacked? Of course, I knew about wool, that it came from the sheep that roamed the hills of home. But wool was for warmth, not the best fabric for this climate. Sheep were no doubt in this country too, but I'd never seen any.

And here we were at the home of where this cotton was grown. I should have known this. Father had owned a woolen mill of which I knew nothing. How would I ever learn how in this country cotton went from seed to fabric? And then, I thought, is this really what I want to do and where I want to be? In the middle of such a desolate area with no one to even be friends with?

"What happens after the cotton is picked?" I ventured, reluctant to even ask, but good manners required polite conversation, so I'd been taught.

"Why we gin it then," he said.

"Gin it," I said, maybe he thought I'd know what he was talking about.

"The cotton gin." He looked over at me and smiled. "You mean you never hear 'bout a cotton gin? Where you been?"

Well, that was a fair question for someone

who knew so little of where things came from or how a seed can be dropped into the ground and produce an entire plant. Truly, I knew of rolling fields of potatoes and various vegetables, but I had never questioned how they were grown or how they made it into our kitchens. Hot tears were welling up.

I was trying, but competing thoughts were winning. I really want to go home. This place is not where I am supposed to be. Why I wondered, could I translate English to Latin and know how to curtsey and make polite conversation with ladies and gentlemen and be adept at embroidering my initials on tea towels and yet know so little? How could I have received all those years of schooling and now realize that not one bit of it was of any use in this wild and untamed land? I had no earthly idea how a tiny seed could be dropped into the ground that would grow to produce the fabric that I wore. For a fleeting second, I thought, Should I really care?

Malachi flicked the reins to keep the old mule moving, while he continued to try to educate me on cotton. I wondered: In this vast uncivilized wilderness, would anyone have any interest or even use for my knowledge of the classics and my skills with embroidery? Then admitted to myself: If truth be known, if I never embroidered another handkerchief or tea towel again, that would be soon enough.

And here was the basic truth: All the skills I'd learned would be of little use now. If I were to be stuck here for any length of time it was going to be far more important to learn how things grew and how the farmer put food on the table. I wanted to care, truly I did, but I had no real interest. Why was this falling on my shoulders?

"Miz," he said, shortening the "Mistress" as he had been using it so often. "Miz, the gin pull them seeds out. Now that be a twofold blessin'," he said. "That gin be invented awhile back. Always before that, them slaves picked that seed out by hand. It take more time than they's got. Tiresome job. But then we take that seed, no matter how it got removed, and store it."

"Aaah," I said, feigning interest, "The seed is then used for next year's crop." This made me feel as though I was at least gaining some small understanding of the life of a farmer. But what would I do with this knowledge? And then I wondered, Why did Damien need seed if it was already here?

"So, we can then use it. Is that correct, Malachi? To plant?" Truly, I wanted to give myself a pat for being so attentive. I swiped at a tear that threatened to drip onto the front of my dress. I hoped he hadn't noticed.

"Yes, Miz. that's the idea. T'ain't perfect, but times like these we's mighty thankful to get it. 'Course this hasn't been much of a year for cotton ..." He let his thoughts trail off.

The fields seemed endless, stretching out almost as far as I could see. "How much land is there, Malachi?" A question I wanted to follow with "And where is the nearest neighbor?" But I held my tongue.

"Well now, when Massa's pap was alive there be close on to 2,000 acres, mostly planted in cotton, some soybeans, some rice, and some time ago, mulberry trees. They was for the silk." He drew a deep breath and continued. "Then Massa's Pap up and died and some was sold off, 'long with a passel of slaves."

"The slaves were sold off?"

"Yup. Not that many left." There was more to this, I was sure. He flicked the whip on the old mule's back. "Git on," he said.

"You got more questions?" he asked. His tone had changed.

I needed to be friends with this fellow, so I continued. "Mulberry trees?" I asked. "Tell me about that." At least I knew what silk was, although I'd never given much thought to where it came from.

He was such a wealth of knowledge and he knew it! There was a half-smile. "For them silkworms." More to try to understand.

He pulled his ever-present hat lower on his forehead, shading his eyes. "You want acreage?" he asked. "Seems like now there be close to 1,000 acres or so. Not 'nuf help to keep it all goin' if you was askin' my opinion. Too much to do, not 'nuf people."

But how do we get more people? I didn't ask that out loud. He wasn't fond of my inquiries into slavery.

"You mentioned silkworms," I said, which seemed to be a safer topic. What I didn't add was what I was thinking to myself: Good Lord! cotton and worms. Life as I'd lived it surely was over.

"Yup, tried that too. Not enuf help. Most of them worms die off. Didn't work out. Still got them mulberry trees. Dey go on forever."

Ahhh, I thought, therefore Mulberry Cove. And no worms! Dare I even think how fortunate it was.

We continued along for over an hour. The constant swaying and hard wooden seat couldn't have been more uncomfortable. Malachi, never seeming at a loss for words, chatted on. He had so much knowledge and history I knew I'd never be able to remember all that he told me.

He said he was trying to skirt the outside boundaries to show me everything. We rode along the side of the creek for a ways, the rhythmic clip-clop of the mule's hooves creating a gentle and soothing sound, nearly putting me to sleep. This was the same road that I'd arrived on not so long ago.

"Why do they call this a creek?" I asked. It seemed to be more like a river.

"Well up not too far, it be more like a creek, gets real narrow. Here 'tis a mite wider. With a good rain, it gets real big."

My thoughts were discouraging: There was too much to learn. Too much to take in of this wild and uncivilized land. So much that I'd never heard of or seen before. And was I really going to need all this information? Long wispy grey tendrils hanging from the trees floated like ghostly wisps in the breeze. He saw me studying it, but I was reluctant to ask. I didn't have to – he said, "Call it Spanish Moss." It had such an eerie look, swaying with every puff of air. It was draped from huge, curved branches keeping much of the interior in darkness. "Use it for mattress stuffin' some. Buggy though. Lotsa things that crawl – gotta be careful."

The wide trees had bent limbs that extended out for nearly twice the height. Malachi said they were live oaks. If I ever climbed a tree those would be the trees with their low and spreading branches that I would have loved to scramble up

We pulled away from the river, the wheels on our cart making crunching noises. A small area of shacks rose up in front of us. Most were in various stages of disarray. "And who lives there?"

"Oh jus' the people."

"What people?"

"Jus' the slave folks."

"Oh really?" I asked. Could this be true? So many in disarray. "I'd like to see where they live if that's all right with you."

"Hmmm!" he said, not committing to anything. He did turn the horse towards the little shantytown. The road between the houses, or shanties – as they weren't really houses – was too narrow for the wagon. Malachi pulled the old mule to a stop and pointed to a few of the cabins. He pointed to where Dancy lived when she didn't stay at the main house, and then where his own shack was, and then pointed out houses that looked to be lived in. He said the names of the people who lived in each shanty. Of course, I knew none of the names he mentioned.

The dirt paths between the shacks were packed hard. There were no footprints. Chickens and two small pigs wandered about. It was very quiet. Each hut had what appeared to be its own small garden plot. Branches had been used to create crude fencing, no doubt meant to keep out foraging animals.

"This is where you all live?" I asked. Malachi nodded his head, He turned the horse away.

England had its poor sections, but I hadn't seen anything quite like this. How could people live here? Live with so little?

"Not many left, not more'n a dozen workers maybe. Cain't do much with that few."

"Where are the people now?" I asked. "Those that are still here?"

"Backfields," he answered. "Time to cut down them weeds 'fore they takes over the entire South." He smiled at his little joke.

"Take me there." And he did.

It took a while with the roughness of the

road, but we came out of a grove of sprawling live oaks. Limbs stretched out in all directions, reaching out for what, I wondered? The ground was littered with Spanish Moss that looked like puffy grey clouds just before a storm.

"There they be," he said, pointing to the workers scattered between the deep furrows.

The field was immense, and the slaves were widely spread out. They all seemed busy with their hoes chopping and slashing. Some wearing tattered straw hats. The women had turbans wrapped around their heads. There were even a couple of small children with child-size hoes.

"Yep," said Malachi before I even asked, "They workin' too. Slashin' at them weeds." One tall man, with his hat pulled low, was taking his time walking down the rows. He was paying close attention to each of the workers, stopping now and again to slap his stick against the palm of his hand. But it was not a stick, it was a whip.

"Who might he be?" I asked, "the one with the whip?"

"That be Damien," Malachi answered, looking like he had more to say, but letting the sentence trail off.

"Oh yes, of course. He came to the house a while back." I hadn't noticed the peg leg. "What exactly does Damien do?" I asked.

"He be the overseer, of course," he answered, which I knew already from the day we first met.

"Tell me about him," I said. After all, if he was working here, I needed to know who he was and where he came from. He didn't appear to be as dark as the others, so I wasn't sure if he too was classified as a slave. He had offered little information, that day not so long ago when I met him in the library.

"He always been here."

"And?" I had the impression that Malachi was reluctant to tell everything there was to know, that there was more information that wasn't being shared.

"He fine," said Malachi. "Been here near forever. Was in the Army some, 'til he got hisself shot up. Worked here 'fore the war."

"Well, he doesn't look like a slave."

"No, he sure don't," said Malachi.

Was this going to be a game we played? I ask and he gives just enough information and no more unless I insist on asking more questions.

"It appears that he has scars on his arms and legs," I said. "I'm sure they're not from the war." I tried to leave it open-ended in hopes that more information would be forthcoming.

"Nope. Not from the war." He flicked the reins on the old mule's back. "Git on," he said.

I turned back to watch a moment longer and, at that very moment, that man with the whip had it raised high in the air. The words couldn't be heard but he was yelling at a slender young boy. Then he brought it down with a loud crack on the boy's legs. A surprised gasp escaped through parched lips. The boy turned and took a step forward. The whip lashed out once more – perhaps without as much power as earlier inflicted, but the crack cut through the air.

"Don't do it Incus," growled the man with the whip. His eyes were slits, his muscles taut and ready for the next blow.

No thought went through my head as I jumped down and stomped to the field. I had seen enough. With no regard for safety, I set out across the mounds of dirt. It was a longer walk than I expected, and he saw me coming.

I tried to yank the whip from his hand, a hand that was embedded with dirt and grime. that looked as though it would never be clean no matter how much scrubbing.

"How dare you." I sputtered. His eyes held

defiance, shock, and deep anger. "Go," I said. "You are dismissed. Don't ever let me see hide nor hair of you again as long as I live."

The anger in his eyes was frightening. Words were choked in his throat. He turned. Anger spilling out of his every pore. The rage in his look surely must be a warning. But I ignored it. He limped off the field, his peg leg slowing his departure. With each step, he left a deep impression of a large footprint and a deep hole. I had little concern for how or where he was going but went to the boy. Blood seeped from the wound across one of his legs.

"Come up in the wagon," I said. "We'll take care of this up at the house." He needed little urging to comply.

The day was over. I'd seen enough.

EIGHT . . .

Freedom was my new friend. Maybe my only friend. At school in England, I had made a few friends, but they came and went according to the wishes and whims of their families. Families that would often decide that they wanted their daughter home instead of so far away. Some of the girls were orphaned like me. Most were there for only one or two years, some for only a few months. Sometimes they were taken away to households in need of a nanny or a tutor or to serve in some capacity in their homes.

My room and board had been taken care of by my aunt and uncle who lived here in South Carolina. It had been paid for from whatever inheritance I had. That is until they decided that I must leave school and come to them at once. I was "needed," said Uncle's letter.

Sister Theresa, the school's head nun, had appeared in my room on that rainy day not so long ago. She knew of the letter and announced that I would be leaving in the morning for Southampton. From there, she proclaimed matter-of-factly, I was to sail to America. I remember only that I couldn't find words. What, I thought, is she saying? The Sister added only that my aunt and uncle had sent for me. And then, like I really wasn't supposed to hear, she mumbled that it was a "sorry business that the funds had run out."

I had left in the morning with my one trunk. Sister Anna waved from the doorway. She was the only one to bid me farewell as I stepped into the carriage that was to take me away. Straining to look back, to say goodbye, I remember how odd it felt to feel nothing. Why did I not have any nostalgic feelings for what had been my home for so long? And why had I not been frightened out of my wits, going off into the unknown?

And then, after boarding the ship bound for America, I felt regret only that I was leaving such a beautiful place, but felt little for the people I was leaving behind. I knew I didn't want to leave all that was familiar. I enjoyed the adventure, what little I knew of it; but at the same time, the unknown felt frightening.

As the ship pulled away from the pier, I remember standing at the railing, staring back at the magnificent country that had been my home. But to miss anyone? I think not. My parents had long been deep in the ground, and I knew of no other living relations other than the aunt who lived in America. My aunt, a total stranger to me, was my mother's only sister. I didn't want to think of it anymore.

And now, here I was in this strange country. Once again, I was alone. But then I did have a new and eager friend. A friend who loved me for no better reason than I was here. Waking in the morning to a furry face that had eyes only for me was more than I could have ever asked. And here he was, looking down on me, his tongue lolling out, with eyes begging me to get up to play. I'd never had a pet before, and this one was so perfect. His long silky black hair was a comfort to me, as I ran my fingers through it.

It had been almost a month since I'd arrived. So much had happened in such a short time. My head still spun thinking of it. So little had been accomplished, and yet so much. Regardless, my fondest desire was still to return to the land of my birth, far away from this very strange inhospitable country. But now, at the very top of the list of the most pressing problems, was finding Uncle Burke. But how I wondered? There wasn't a way that I knew of.

Today, however, I resolved to get through some of those stacks of paper. Maybe, just maybe, I would find an answer in there as to his whereabouts. It was daunting. The piles had the look of the mounds of hay that covered the rolling farmlands in the fall at harvest time. But those piles of hay may have been far neater than what covered the surface of this desk.

I recalled seeing one unopened letter lying near the top of one of the ready-to-topple piles. Should I open it? I wondered. Not sure that it was my business, but what to do? There was no one else to tend to it.

The letter was addressed to Aunt Jane. There was no return address on the envelope. Carefully, I lifted the flap, hoping that something inside would provide a clue as to the whereabouts of Uncle Burke.

And it did! The signature was his. The letter said little, not even inquiring about Aunt Jane's well-being. He wrote that he had been in a few gun battles but that he was well. His company was heading out and should arrive in Virginia within a week. But the letter wasn't dated and there weren't more than three sentences. There was, however, an address under his signature.

An address in Virginia.

I wrote back at once. There was so much to say. I had arrived. Aunt Jane had unexpectedly and sadly died, and I now found myself in the position of running his farm. Plantation, I should say. The word still would not come easily to me. I was accustomed to the rolling farms and broad estates of England. But, I inquired of the Uncle what should be done and how I might help. I would post the letter with all due haste with the assistance of Malachi, who would know how to handle such things.

That was just one letter from the top of one of the piles. So much more to be attended to. I was sure there would be lots more still to discover. The drawers were nearly empty as I went through one last time. That was when I discovered a heavy metal box. It was tucked way in the back of one of the bottom drawers.

It was securely locked with no key to be found.

I enlisted the help of Malachi. He handed me a hammer. With one good whack, I broke the metal lock. Lifting the lid, I was rewarded with even more disheveled papers. But at the very bottom of the pile was an envelope holding a few coins – some silver, some gold.

There wasn't much, but it would, with luck, be enough to buy the seed that was needed and perhaps a few other things. If I could somehow get to the village, I could purchase whatever Malachi thought necessary and take care of the few household things.

Seed should have been uppermost on my list, but my thoughts were of tea. For far too long I had been sipping the bland brew that these Americans thought was tea. And, according to Dancy, we were out of sugar, flour, and salt. Her way of informing me was unique, to be sure. When I'd asked for sugar for my bitter-tasting coffee, which seemed to be a favorite of the Americans, she merely said "T'ain't none." It was the same when I mentioned that there was no bread on the table, "T'ain't none."

Did she not have a vocabulary? Could she speak more than two-word sentences? I wondered. She obviously was not fond of me and was overworked by this huge house that, in truth, no one person could ever keep up. But, what to do about it? I wasn't sure.

By week's end, I had grown positively anxious to ride into town just to be away for awhile. And we did! The trip took half the day! The rains of the late spring that the cotton seedlings loved so much had turned the road into a quagmire of mud. The wheels of the wagon sank more than once, and I had about decided that we needed to turn around when Malachi said that town was just a bit further.

Having little knowledge of driving a wagon and controlling a mule, I had pressed Malachi into service. Regardless of his limited sight, he knew his way to town. There was not another body that could be spared at this busy time of year. Almost blind or not, he knew every turn and every landmark along the way, pointing out this and that as we rolled along the shores of Mulberry Creek.

I was glad that we were becoming friends. He, after all, knew more than anyone else on the property.

"How much land is there. Where does it end?" I was busy trying to take in everything I was seeing.

He pointed to an ancient tree, bent from the weight of too many branches. "That old tree. That be the end of the property." The length and breadth of the acreage was almost beyond imagining. How could one landowner own this much or keep it up?

"And why is it that we don't plant down

here?" I asked.

"No help," he answered. "Cain't spare them workers. Too much to do in them cotton fields." This seemed logical enough, but then why have so much land?

"This be lowland," he continued. "Had it in rice a while back."

"Rice?" I questioned.

"That be right. Massa have too much other work to keep up with it. Needs more help to work them rice fields."

"How much more help?" I asked, having no idea on this earth how one grows rice.

"Takes a certain kind a slave to do it. Massa had them Gullahs plantin' and harvestin' but then Massa Stephens come in and offered to buy the lot o' them Gullahs for his plantation."

"So, he sold them?"

"That be right. Only them Gullahs knows how to work the rice – no one else any good at it. So, fields dry up and rice go 'way."

"Indeed," I said, "So they just up and sell people?" I shook my head in near disbelief, "When they no longer need them?"

He did not answer the question but slapped the reins to keep the mule moving forward.

"What, then," I asked, "is a Gullah?"

He gave me a critical eye, as though I were a child, but he did give me an answer: "They be the low country Negras. They know what they's about when it comes to rice growin'. Cain't understand a word they say what wif' their own language and all."

"So why aren't they here?"

"Most sold to Massa Stephens. But others run off, back to the coast. It still be low country but more wet." At least I knew what the low country was; we were in it. It was swampy and mosquito-infested. Much of the rest of this plantation was on what Malachi referred to as the "high ground."

He flicked the reins. The mule was tiring. "He not real good to his nigras so most glad to move on."

"What are you saying?" I asked.

Malachi raised an eyebrow. His clouded eyes were questioning. "You seen them stripes," it was a statement, not a question. Again, I had that dumbfounded look. "All over the legs an' arms of most of that help."

"Oh Lord!" was all I could think. Was it really true? But Malachi had shut down. He was deaf to my continuing questions, focusing solely on the progress of the mule.

Then what to do? A while back we had passed what appeared to be overgrown fields carved into squares with straight ditches between them. Old rice fields? I wondered. That must be what I'd seen. Would it be possible? Could this low land be returned to rice fields? This would take more thought and far more information than Malachi was providing. And then I remembered. This was not part of my plan. More than anything I wanted to return to England. I did not want to get involved in the life of an American plantation.

The bumpy road was coming to an end. The seed store was just ahead. The boards creaked as we entered. The shop dark. One lone window allowed a minimum of light. Few people were shopping. Although Malachi couldn't see, he knew exactly what we needed and directed the boy who offered to help us.

Malachi then introduced me to a Mr. Brown, telling him that I was the new mistress of Mulberry Cove. An old fellow, friendly enough, Mr. Brown raised his eyebrows and his crinkled old eyes inspected me from head to toe. I think I saw the beginning of a disbelieving smile.

"What would you like?" he asked, not unkindly. Dancy had put in a few requests – something like if we ever planned to eat again, we might want to purchase some flour and corn-meal and a few other victuals.

There wasn't enough money.

I looked for Malachi to take him outside so's we could have a chat, but he was nowhere to be seen. American money baffled me, but then so did the English pound, as I rarely had occasion to use it.

Mr. Brown tried to explain that what with the war and all, he rarely extended any credit. He also mentioned that he had extended credit – more often than he would have liked – to my aunt and uncle and that there was still an out-standing amount due.

My cheeks were no doubt flaming red. My embarrassment was so great that if Malachi had been anywhere within reach, I would have jumped in the wagon and headed for home, never to be seen in this town again. But where was he?

"Why, Miss Amelia," said a voice at my side. "What a very pleasant surprise." I knew no one in this strange and foreign country but turned in response to the voice. It was Mr. Billingsley from the ship, from my trip across the Atlantic.

I hardly remembered his name and was none too pleased that he was here witnessing my distress. Greeting him with less enthusiasm than was proper, I made my apologies at the same time.

"Tis a pleasure," I said, "But my man is holding the wagon for me, and I really must be on my way."

"Well please, let me carry these few purchases," he said, picking up my basket. He and Mr. Brown exchanged knowing looks. Mr. Brown sighed, shook his head, and walked away.

Not sure of an appropriate response in this circumstance, but certainly not wanting Mr. Billingsley to know of my business, I nodded and led the way out of the store.

"Miss Fitzgibbons," he began, "I couldn't help but hear the discussion with Mr. Brown regarding the credit situation at Mulberry Cove." His voice was low as if we were two conspirators. "Mr. Brown and I have an understanding, and I've taken care of things. But I wonder if I might be of further assistance?"

A flush of embarrassment was creeping up, no doubt turning my cheeks a flaming red. At the same time, I was running out of patience. My answer was less than grateful. "Indeed," I answered. "And why would you be wanting to do that?" My voice was tight and unfriendly. I hadn't meant to sound quite so ungrateful, especially if Mr. Billingsley had in truth helped with the financial situation.

"Only to assist one so young," he said. I truly did not believe what he was saying and had a feeling that I was to be an object of his attention if I so much as gave him a smile.

"I thank you, Mr. Billingsley, but that won't be necessary."

"I assure you, Miss Fitzgibbons, I have nothing more in mind than lending a bit of assistance during these trying times." He harrumphed a bit, cleared his throat, and then continued. "I knew your aunt," he said.

"Aunt Jane?" I asked.

"Well, yes," he answered. I sensed an evasiveness in his voice. "If you would care to accompany me to the hotel just over there," he said, pointing to a large building across the way. "It would be my pleasure to treat you to a cup of tea and maybe a biscuit if they're still to be had."

My tummy had been growling for an hour and the temptation of food was overwhelming, although good judgment said no.

"Thank you, I'll accept your invitation." Hunger won out. Besides, I reasoned, it was daylight and there were other people in town, it was a public room, and Malachi would be watching for me.

Mr. Billingsley nodded his approval and tried to take my arm to guide me. I chose to walk under my own power. It did involve lifting my already soiled skirt and petticoat while stepping over and around deep ruts and foul-smelling puddles. The path to the hotel was slippery, and mud weighed down my boots.

"My dear child," he said, "Thank you for joining me," We were seated at a very small table close to the window.

I bristled. Why was he calling me a child? Those days had been left behind when I departed my homeland. My annoyance must have been evident.

"The braids," he said. "They're not often seen on the mistress of a plantation."

I was taken aback not only by his comment on how I wore my hair but there it was again — that word: Mistress. The tea arrived just in time to stop me from making any comment. My fingers aimlessly stroked one of my long braids, held in place by my bonnet. What made them so offensive? I wondered.

Mr. Billingsley continued, as though nothing

were amiss. "I have a tale to tell." He came just short of blowing on his cup of steaming and fragrant tea, a gesture I had seen only here in America. Nevertheless, he continued. "I was close to your aunt when she first came to this country. Your uncle was a cantankerous sort, and your aunt needed a bit of support now and again." He paused for a moment as if giving thought to whether or not he should continue. "You do resemble her, by the way. The almost blonde hair and the blue eyes and of course the height. I believe you are a bit taller than she was." He looked away for a moment and then continued. "There is more to this than I will discuss today, but I had tried to assist where I could, as she and I became acquainted when she first crossed the Atlantic. She was to join your uncle."

He sipped his tea with caution. It was piping hot, the steam rising in curls above the china cup. He blew at the hot liquid, lacking the patience to let it cool. "I continued with my travels. On one excursion a few years after Jane had settled here, an unfortunate incident took place." He set his cup down. A great sigh escaped before he continued. "At Jane's request, I had accompanied their son James who was to attend school in England. He was the only son and quite young. They felt that it would be more advantageous to his future to send him to his mother's homeland for his education."

He sighed and then took a cautious sip of his tea. He stared out the window for a bit before he continued. "James was his name. Most unfortunately, through no one's fault, he died on the voyage over. Probably consumption. He was our, or rather their, only son." Oh my! I thought. Had he truly said, "our" before he said, "their"? His shoulders slumped, and sadness clouded his eyes.

He took a moment to continue. "Regardless, your Aunt Jane did not hold me accountable and was always very kind to me. We had become very close on her initial trip to America." He stopped for a moment to gaze out the window. "I shall never forget her graciousness toward me. And as I had mentioned, I had tried to be of assistance while she was alive, but there were many obstacles." He paused again. "There is more, but I believe we've covered enough for one day."

He had piqued my curiosity. Why had I never known that my aunt and uncle had a son?

But, now I could see Malachi through the window. The afternoon sun was descending in the western sky. It was time for our return trip home. There was more to this tale, I was sure, but it would have to wait for another day.

NINE . . .

Mr. Billingsley and his chat about my aunt had piqued my curiosity. Perhaps I would get to hear more someday. Life on a plantation, I was quickly learning, does not slow down, take a holiday, or stop for anything.

Malachi came up on the porch, his hat in hand. His appearance on the porch was not unusual; it seemed that's where we met most times when he had one thing or another that needed to be discussed.

"Somethin's not right," he said, and for all the world, it looked as though he was sniffing the air. He said he felt it in his very bones. His nearly blind eyes were searching, squinting up, trying to see the sky. He twisted his old wool hat around in his hands, stretching it in one direction and then another.

"Listen," he said. His head was cocked as if trying to pick up sounds in the air. "Hear that?" I tried to hear what he was hearing, but nothing came to me. "Birds," he said.

"But I can't hear any."

"That be the problem. No birds. Air is still." And it was. It was heavy and thick.

It was late August, and I had never been through a heat that could compare to that in America's South. It was so thick with moisture; it was as if one breathed underwater. Even when I wore my thinnest cotton frock -that had, in truth, gotten a bit short, there was little relief. I wondered, for the hundredth time: Would I ever become accustomed to this strange land?

I had discovered early on that in heat like this, it was necessary to move slowly to avoid becoming drenched in dampness. I never had much use for a handkerchief, but now I kept one handy, forever mopping up the drips trickling down my forehead.

I listened again. There had always been birds, the ever-present call of the mockingbird, the flash of bright red as a cardinal flew by, and the raucous caw of the blue jay. But today there was nothing other than the soft buzz of a honeybee. Even that noise seemed subdued.

"What are you saying, Malachi?" I asked.

"I'm thinkin' we got ourselves some weather comin' in."

"What are you talking about?"

"Feels like there's a blow comin' on."

I stood for a bit trying to feel what it was that he was feeling or hearing or seeing. There was nothing except the usual afternoon heaviness that preceded our almost daily thunder-and-lightning storms. It had taken more than awhile to become accustomed to, but now I almost looked forward to the violent crack and flash of lightning and the booms and crash of thunder that shook the very walls. It would bring a bit of temporary coolness. I hadn't been quite so fearless when the first of these many storms had crept up on me. I had cowered in fear, thinking the world was ending. Never had I heard such noise or seen such brilliant flashes of light. And that, oddly, was the first time that I saw Dancy allow a smile to sneak up on her usual unhappy face. She was amused by my ignorance. And I wondered, for the hundredth time, was there nothing this girl liked about me?

The cooling rains truly were something to look forward to, but windstorms still frightened me. The afternoon storms were actually a welcome respite from the nearly unbearable heat of late-day August. The downpour of rain would cool things temporarily before the earth would steam again in the summer heat.

Malachi interrupted my thinking. "If it be comin' it be comin' soon," he said.

"Indeed," I said. "Then what should we do?"

"T'ain't much to do," he answered. "Jus' got to ride it out." He turned, without so much as a by-your-leave, and headed down the stairs.

He was right. We were not about to experience our usual late afternoon thunderstorm. Instead, a breeze began to pick up. At first lightly, just touching the tops of the mighty magnolias and sprawling live oaks.

This was not a good thing, I thought, as memories – unwanted – crowded in.

I tried to push them aside, but visions of Gwendolyn telling me that my parents would not be returning prevailed, and still haunted me. Gwendolyn had been my governess for as long as I could remember. I was so young. Wearing her crisp gray-and-white uniform she had entered my room. She sat on the edge of the bed. Gwendolyn was all business and never sat down. And then in her usual abrupt manner, she proceeded to give me only the brutal facts: My parent's shay, she said, had overturned. There had been a terrible windstorm off the Atlantic that blew down everything in its path.

The road that they were traveling had washed out, and the shay had gone over the edge. It had gone over the edge – with my mother and father.

We had felt that storm at home. It had rattled all the windows throughout the night. Gwendolyn said that my father, with Mum in the back of the shay, had been trying to stay ahead of the storm. He wanted desperately to get back home.

But it wasn't to be. The shay – a dastardly American invention, wasn't meant to be driven through a violent rainstorm; it was meant for Sunday drives in the country, or so said Gwendolyn.

"But when will they come home?" I asked. My mind was too young to understand what she had told me. She said no more. That was all I was to learn from her.

~

And here I stood in a strange land. A windstorm brewing along the horizon. A mist started to blow in the breeze. The sky was quickly becoming very dark with roiling thunderheads. The air felt strange. The wind changed. No longer was it a gusty light breeze, but a strong, steady blow coming from one direction. For a moment, my skirt caught up in the breeze, wrapping tightly around my legs. I struggled to stay upright.

I wanted to hide – fear of windstorms forever with me. Thoughts of that terrible blow that had sprung up from nowhere all those many years ago and taken all that I'd ever known and loved, would always be with me. That event had changed my life forever. It was frightening. Now I felt danger, but where could I go?

The wind was nearly howling. The intensity was frightening. It felt as though it could pick me up and send me sailing off the porch. I clung to a pillar, flecks of aged paint stuck to my hands. Where to hide?

And then there was Malachi, struggling through the roaring wind and falling darkness. With him were two men I hadn't seen before; they nodded a quick greeting. Together the three fought the wind to close our shutters. They had been banging back and forth, coming very close to being torn loose in the gale. Two held them closed while the third dropped the long board to hold them securely. Branches were snapping in the wind. I watched as a huge limb from a grand old magnolia snapped off like a twig and went crashing to the ground.

Malachi was making his way down the porch stairs with the assistance of the two others. He turned back for a moment, and I thought he yelled, "I be back." I shrieked into the storm "Come in!" But my words were snatched away into the storm. The three men were already disappearing down the drive.

There was nothing to do but go back inside the house. I could barely steady myself to push the front door open.

The house was filled with darkness. My only thoughts were: Where is Dancy and what of the slaves down in the shacks? The wind began to screech and soon became a continuous howl. I imagined it to be what a banshee, that mythical Irish creature, must sound like. But this sound was real, and it seemed to be getting louder.

Wandering from room to room trying to think of what to do, I was feeling terribly alone in this big house. It was very dark and very eerie. Where was Dancy? Freedom trotted along behind me. His head was hanging down. An occasional whimper escaped as his dark eyes peered up at me.

"Free, I don't know what to do." My fingers

reached for the smoothness of the familiar dark fur. "Where is everyone?" Before I even thought, I pulled my wrap around me and went back outside. Freedom whined to come with me. "No, you stay. This wind could carry you off to kingdom come."

Leaning for a moment against the brick wall to keep out of the wind, I tried to create a plan, thinking: I do not want to stay in the big house alone. And Shantytown may not be safe if the river were to rise. If I stick close to the trees that shelter the drive, I could get down there and bring everyone up to the house – if anything was left of it.

For a moment I stared in disbelief into the thick rain-soaked air as leaves and branches blew about. Branches snapped, and leaves were stripped from trees, clogging the air with debris. The wind howled, almost screaming. It was difficult to stay upright.

The walk down the drive took far too long as I zigzagged between the trees, trying to stay sheltered. Cracks shot through the air as limbs were snapped off by the shrieking wind. I tried to keep a sharp eye out for where they were falling. There were so many ear-splitting crashes from the branches, I wondered if there would be anything left.

And then a tremendous crack just above me and the rustle of a falling limb. Shivers ran up my spine as an overly large magnolia branch landed in the exact spot where I had just stood. Goosebumps ran up my arms, and I shivered.

Staying upright was not easy as the wind threatened to either carry me off or topple me over.

It took forever to get down to Shantytown. The row of tired, dilapidated, and shabby shacks had the look of an abandoned ghost town. There was not a person or child or dog to be seen – only splintered branches being blown along the hard-packed, now-slippery path.

Certain that the largest shack belonged to Malachi, I ran – more like lurched toward it, as it was difficult to stay upright. I had nearly reached the door when I realized I was sloshing through water. Just as I had feared, Mulberry Creek was overflowing its banks. Floodwater was rising rapidly and was already over my ankles.

The door to the old shack that may have been Malachi's wouldn't open. I beat on it, but there was no response. The roar of the wind carried off the racket of my pounding. Fearing I was going to be picked up and blown away – or worse, washed away – I clung to the splintery door and squinted into the gloom. Debris flew through the air. Although it was nearly impossible to see, I squinted to view the row of tumbledown shacks. And then, in the row on the opposite side of the path, I spotted a shack with a door partially opened. Through the open slot an arm was waving.

The wind was at my back. It wanted to pick me up or blow me over, I wasn't sure which. I crept along the row of shacks, one hand grabbing at anything so I wouldn't be blown into the great unknown.

A torrent of thoughts came to me: I could very well be carried off by the wind and deposited into the river, never to be seen again. Would anyone miss me, or know what happened – or even care? Maybe this wasn't what I should have done. But then, without warning, a very strong, dark hand wrapped around my arm. I froze in fear as it pulled me through the doorway. My drenched skirt encased my legs like a second skin, nearly tripping me. I was truly confused. Who had grabbed me?

A stool was pulled up behind me and hands pushed me to sit. Warm as the day had been, cold now shook me; I was soaked to the very bone. It took a moment to adjust to the eerie, near-darkness in the hut. Three young girls stood in front of me. I was still gasping but asked where the others were.

They shook their heads. "Didn't come in from da' fields," one answered.

Off in a darkened corner were two very young children sitting on a blanket. One was shivering. I got up and went to pick the child up, realizing I was probably shivering too. But his big eyes hadn't left me since I'd been pulled through the door.

A threadbare blanket was thrown over our shoulders. I asked the girls if they knew of the whereabouts of Dancy. There was no answer. All three stood, fidgeting, unsure of what to do.

The tallest of the group jerked her head in the direction of the river.

"What do you mean?" I asked. "Are you saying Dancy is down at the river?"

"Yes'm," she said. And then I listened. The wind had died down to almost nothing. How could that happen? I was nearly killed half an hour ago by falling branches. Was the storm over? Sunbeams began streaming through the cracks between the boards that made up the walls. I peeked out the door. Can it be? I thought. The sun was actually coming out. What has happened?

I turned back to the girls. "Well then, where exactly is Dancy?"

Looks were exchanged between them. "Where is she?" I asked more insistently, looking at them more closely. They were all far too thin. They may have been close to my age. All wore some sort of sack-type dress of the most basic homespun. It looked like tow, a flimsy combination of cotton and linen. It was very itchy. Why didn't they have proper clothing?

A thought passed through my head: Had I ever even seen these girls before? People worked here, and I had no idea who they were or what they did.

"Why?" I asked while attempting to warm the young child I was holding. I tried to get a better look at who I was speaking to.

"Damien 'sposed to be comin' to git her."

"Good Lord," I said, "Damien doesn't work here anymore." But then I thought, could it be that Dancy had an interest in him? How could that be? And why didn't I know this?

But more importantly, it finally occurred to me, Why was I having this conversation, while the water was rising around our very feet. The sun was streaming down, but we could all very well drown while we chatted.

"He be her frien' from down da' way."

"Yes, I know who Damien is," I said, hoping not to sound harsh.

"'You know 'bout the frien'?"

This conversation wasn't going well.

"Did she go down to the pier?" I asked.

"Yes'm," said the one who was twirling the hem of her dress around her finger. She was a strong-looking young girl, thin as she was, who couldn't have been any older than I was.

A shiver went up my spine. Why would Dancy do that? But then I thought, Maybe that was why she was so often absent from the house at night.

We stood outside for a moment in the warmth of the sunbeams that were streaming down. "Can you take these children up to the house?" I asked the tallest girl. "The water may get higher."

She seemed to want to say something, but she only kept looking at her feet. "What is it?" I asked. I sensed that she might be so hesitant to speak because maybe we'd never seen each other before. She didn't answer.

"Then go now. These shacks aren't going to

take too much more of this." And as if to prove what I was saying, a loose shingle fell from the roof and clattered down the side of the shanty.

And then there was Malachi.

"Where in heaven's name have you been?" I asked, not meaning to sound so cross.

"Miz, gotta tend to them livestock and chase down some o' those tryin' to git away."

"What are you talking about?" I asked.

"Some of them field hands think this be a good time to move on."

This was going to take more explaining than I had time for.

"Malachi, get these people up to the house where they can get warm. And see to the damage. How can it be repaired?"

"Ma'am," he started again. "There's gonna be more. And it's gonna be lots worse. And it's gonna be sooner than you gonna like." What on earth was he talking about I wondered. I'm sure that my look of confusion, must have made me look like the village dunce.

"Ma'am, this be a hurricane. This be what they calls the eye."

Good heavens! I thought. Yes, I knew about windstorms although hurricanes weren't part of England's weather and yes, I'd read somewhere about the eye – but I must have had a blank look as he went on.

"It be comin' back lots worse. There be a whole other side to dis storm." I had no choice but to believe him.

"Well then, quick! Get these people up to the house. I'll go down to the dock to try to find Dancy. Now go on," I said shooing him with my hand.

He started to object and was actually raising his voice at me, but already I was too far away to hear whatever he had to say.

TEN . . .

The pier wasn't far from Shantytown, but it could well have been across the ocean for the trouble it would take to get there. Staying close to the shacks, I stumbled and all but crawled through the rising water. The wind was starting to whip up again and was soon even more ferocious than before.

But back to thinking about Dancy: What if she'd already gone? What if she wasn't there? I should go back to the house. This was foolish, chasing after a girl who was determined to meet someone who well may not be there, or who may have already been spirited off to some far-off place. And was it really Damien who she was meeting? The rain was back with a vengeance. The wind and the pelting, stinging rain, kept me bent over.

I knew I was almost there when I saw the pilings. They were sticking up out of the swirling water like dark fingers reaching for the sky.

Muddy, sloshing water kept the pier from view. The lazy Mulberry Creek had become a wild torrent of churning, angry water, which had already overflowed both banks of the creek.

The wharf jutted out into the river. It was where they loaded the bales of cotton for market. The roiling torrent of raging water threatened to sweep the pier away. I could see branches and logs and all sorts of debris careening down the river, with some heaping up against the shore. But there was also an odd-looking something that caught my eye. It looked like a broken branch with a rag thrown against it. It was nearly impossible to see it more clearly in the driving rain.

Choosing my footing with great care, I walked through the swirling water onto the pier which felt rickety, as though it might topple at any moment.

But there was something there. A tossed-aside piece of cloth caught up in a tree branch, maybe?

But it was not a rag. It was Dancy! And good grief, both her arms were wrapped tightly around the huge, crooked branch of what must have been an entire tree. I could see the jagged roots sticking up in the air, rising above the churning flood.

The water continued to rise, as it continued to breach both banks. It seemed that Dancy's body had been thrown against a tree. She appeared to be clinging to a branch in a desperate fight to stay afloat. How she had come to be there was going to be anyone's guess. Although I tried, I could not tell if she was even still alive.

And then, she looked over at me! Her dark eyes were dazed, appearing frozen in time. How could I get to her? I had no idea. There was a flatboat, which was far too large for me to handle, but the skiff was still there. Maybe I could manage that. It was bobbing like a cork on the top of the raging river. What to do?

Dancy's eyes weren't focusing; her lids were only half-open. Near panic, I thought: I could run for help – but help from whom, and from where? Dancy, will not survive much longer if I don't do something soon!

The water was now up to my knees, the wind was howling with a sound I'd never heard before. I screamed "Hang on!" to deaf ears.

Dancy showed no recognition. Debris flew through the air, branches, leaves, and shingles. The crack of more branches being torn from the trees was splitting the air. My skirt was threatening to trip me as it wrapped around my ankles, the weight of it pulling me down.

How could I ever guide a boat through this? Before I thought it out, my hands were pulling in the rope. The skiff came up next to me and I leaped over the side into it. There was nothing proper about the way that I landed at the bottom of that boat, and I had nearly knocked myself out when my head hit the gunnel. I shook it off and tried to focus.

The oars were there, tucked under the seats. How much good they would do couldn't even be imagined. A huge *snap* split through the howl of the wind and I watched as Dancy and the limb that she was clinging to started to float down the river.

The decision was made for me! The rope holding the boat broke. The skiff began its perilous journey down the once lazy Mulberry Creek, unrecognizable in its flooded state. I could make sense of nothing: Where was this wind coming from? Why had it changed so quickly? And how was Dancy hanging on to that limb? The water was crashing over her. It was also threatening to sink me in the little skiff. The river and the wind and water were at least pushing us in the same direction. Within minutes, the roaring torrent narrowed. The branch caught on something. Dancy was still, the water swirled around her.

There was no directing which way my skiff would go. At any moment it would capsize, I was sure of it. There were oars but they were useless against the raging current. A sudden burst of wind blew the skiff toward the very branch that Dancy was clinging to. My bonnet flew off to Kingdom come. The skiff tangled in the branch. Wrestling with the rope, I found it impossible to tie it to the broken limb.

"Dancy, don't you dare let go!" I screamed into the wind. I had her by one arm, fighting with the current. Pulling her over to the side of the boat, I yanked and tugged and with one final effort got her over the side and into the boat. The branch began to shift. We were being dragged farther down the river. There was no way to guide us to the shore.

I screamed at the wind, I'm not sure what words came out, but I'm sure they weren't the words of a lady. It didn't matter. The wind snatched the words from my mouth, tossing them to who knows where. The branch twisted and lodged our boat against another fallen tree. The rope holding us to the branch snapped. We were now firmly entrapped by the gnarled and sprawling skeleton of a trunk that had once been one of the ancient oaks that lined the river.

We had taken on far too much water, but there was no way to bail it out or to get free of the entanglement. We were in the skiff, trapped in the snarl of bent and unyielding branches.

Leaning over Dancy's still body I yelled, trying to be heard over the scream of the wind, "Dancy, wake up!" Her skin was grey and icy, her eyes half-opened. It was hard to tell if she was still alive.

"Wake up!" I yelled again and slapped her cheeks. "You've got to help me." A shiver sent a shock through her body. Garbled words were snatched into the air. "C'mon," I said, "we've got to get out of this boat or we're both going to drown." Struggling mightily, she righted herself to a sitting position and leaned against the splintered side of the skiff.

Jamming an oar down into the water, I discovered that it wasn't very deep. If we could make our way through all the broken branches, we could get to the shore.

And then it happened. How I still cannot say. But from what Dancy later told me, my skirt tangled around my legs, and I fell overboard. She said I was dragged under by a rope that had wrapped around my legs. I knew only that I was underwater, and I was very possibly drowning. Later she told me she thought I was gone. My hair was tangled and spreading out everywhere in the water and that was what she grabbed. She said she actually got a handful and used that to bring me up from down in the depths. I do remember sputtering and then throwing up a good deal of water. She wasn't able to pull me into the boat but instead got into the water alongside me. Shaky as she was, she was trying to keep both of us from being swept away.

We were close to the shore. I could see it and the water wasn't that deep. But I couldn't stand. Dancy was dragging me. The current wanted to pull us into the raging torrent. I was sure we were both going to be swept away. The tree that kept us from being pulled down the river began to shift. It was ready to continue its way down the rushing swirl of water.

Dancy, her eyes still dazed, grabbed a handful of my dress and wouldn't let go. She pulled me to the shore. I tried to help but my feet kept sinking in the squishy bottom. We hung onto the branches trying to keep from being washed down the river. It was hard to tell who was dragging who as the rush of water fought to pull us down. There was no way but to crawl for the last few feet. My skirt wrapped tightly around my legs and ripped in protest to the sopping tangle. We inched our way out of the deadly rush of water. Unable to stand, we collapsed in the mud.

The rain was pouring down and blowing so hard that it hurt. It felt like thousands of tiny pebbles were pounding us, trying to beat us down. The wind was threatening to pick us up and toss us back into the water. Dancy's dark eyes were threatening to close.

"Don't you dare," I said. "You've got to help me," I shook her. "Stand if you can."

She tried to focus, but there didn't seem to be much recognition. But then she stood. Not well. She was shaky but pulled me up, keeping her arm around my waist to keep me upright. Together we struggled to stay on our feet. We slipped and slid our way over to the embankment. Looking up I thought, we can't do this. It looked impossible.

A steep, muddy slope was in front of us. It was slippery and it was quickly deteriorating, plops of mud sliding down the side. Dancy took the lead but it was hard to tell who was pulling and who was pushing. It wasn't very steep and roots jutted out, some giving a handhold but others threatening to trip us. Rushing streams of water washed down the steep embankment pulling clods of dirt and debris with it, wanting to wash us back into the river, hampering our progress. It felt like hours, but reaching the top, we regained our footing. Dancy had to pull me up and over the last ridge. My strength had given out. We stood with our arms around each other, not sure if we should cheer or cry. I squinted into the gloom. We were far from home, I was sure of it. Dancy looked dazed but I asked her anyway. "Which way?"

The road was a quagmire of mud, water filling every rut. She pointed in the direction from where the stream was flowing. I hoped she was right. Taking a few steps, she barely nodded. I hoped that meant we were headed the right way.

Surely it was going to be a long walk, but there was no other plan. We leaned heavily on each other, inching our way forward, trying to put one foot in front of the other, our progress painfully slow. She handed me a broken, but almost smooth branch to use for a walking stick. Debris was flying through the air and more than once we had to step out of the way of a falling branch. Many of the trees had been ripped free of all their glossy green leaves. On some, only a skeleton of brown twisted branches remained.

Our clothes, heavy with river water and soaking rain, stuck to our legs and weighed us down. It felt as though we'd been walking for hours, but in fact, it had probably been only minutes since getting up to the road.

"Dancy," I said, my voice raspy, "Please speak to me. Let me know you're all right."

"For sure," she mumbled. I was crying. It may have been more like a howl than something one did while dabbing at teary eyes with a neatly pressed and embroidered handkerchief. But it just wouldn't stop. The fright of what we'd been through!

Dancy was murmuring words that were being snatched by the wind, but she was also patting my back and holding me up. My legs were threatening to collapse. She put my head on her shoulder and said over and over "It be all right. It be all right." I was sobbing and I think I was saying all sorts of unkind things about what I thought of America and the South and their war and their dastardly weather and how much I yearned to go home. Most of it was garbled. Was this to be my end?

And then – something was coming toward us. Dancy put a hand over my mouth, silencing further words of complaint. It was difficult to make out just what it was that was emerging from the deep and swirling mist. I didn't even care! We could hide or we could stand there. Maybe we would get trampled by a tribe of the wild Indians that the Americans so liked to talk about, or maybe be attacked by a pack of hungry wolves. A thousand thoughts were swirling through my mind, each scarier than the last. But truly we were both so close to collapsing that it no longer seemed to matter.

Dancy yelled "Help!" Her words, I'm sure, were flung into the wind. Scanning the trees and branches at the sides of the road, I thought perhaps we could run and hide. But then I realized that my feet wouldn't move. But maybe, just maybe, it wasn't a herd of wild beasts but rather someone who would come to our aid. If not, we would have to live with whatever the outcome. We were smack in the middle of the road, Dancy had pulled me down, fearing no doubt that I was going to topple over. We were sitting on a fallen tree; her arm stayed around my waist, keeping me upright. Whoever or whatever it was that was coming out of the swirling fog and driving rain would have to mow us down or eat us. We had no strength left to get out of the way.

But then appeared the most welcome sight of my life: People mounted on horseback. They were coming straight toward us. They hadn't seen us in the gloom. Their horses were ready to jump the fallen tree when one reared up on his hind legs, his powerful hooves pawing the air. He nearly threw his rider. "Halt!" was all I heard.

Then, "What the ____ ?" They stared down at us.

Soldiers. It was difficult to tell how many there were, or if they were Yankees or Confederates. I didn't care. They sat astride their horses, each more soaked and miserable than the other, their uniforms so disheveled, it was hard to tell if they were blue or grey.

The lead fellow, looking a bit confused or maybe questioning what he was seeing, dismounted. He reached out and grabbed my arm, maybe to see if we were real? I let out a yelp. Dancy stood, putting an arm out as if to protect me, ready to take issue with anyone who touched us. But there was no need. I do believe that I no longer cared if they trampled us, ate us, or left us for dead.

"Who are you?" asked a voice whose words were nearly muted by the wind. "Lands sake," said another, "It's two women."

Hardly aware of what was happening; I felt strong hands pushing me up onto a saddle. I felt, more than saw, a fellow swing up behind me. "There now, you'll be fine," he said, trying not to yell to be heard over the screaming of the wind. "Your girl is on the other horse," he yelled. "Look what you've done to her. She's almost dead." I wasn't sure if I had heard him correctly. "Why don't you take care of your people?"

My mind couldn't understand what he was saying. He held me tightly around the waist and spoke into my ear. "There's a house down the way. We'll get you there. Probably take a while." He flicked his reins, "Trees and branches everywhere. I've never seen the like," he said.

I was dazed, my head felt fuzzy, and it was difficult to follow what he was saying. He had tried to share his jacket, opening it up and wrapping it around me. It was sopping and only the warmth of his body offered any protection.

After what may well have been hours, and a very lengthy and uncomfortable ride, he had us back to the big house. It was our house.

My arms and legs were so stiff they wouldn't bend. My hair, long ago having come undone, was sopping and so tangled, a brush may never get through it. Hands belonging to people I didn't know brought me up the stairs and through the porch and settled us, both wrapped in a huge blanket, on the sofa. A crackling fire was lit, warming the room and giving it a cheery glow. As much as I tried to follow what was happening, I dozed off, having no idea or even caring who had brought us back and settled us in. Settled us in for whatever was next.

ELEVEN . . .

They were far more frightened than I was. They were gathered in the huge kitchen, most sitting on the floor. These were the very people who kept this plantation running, and I knew so few of them. Their dark eyes followed my every move. They were hungry, cold, and tired.Where to start. I was still having difficulty walking or talking – not sure if it was the fright or the aching in my very bones that wouldn't let go. Despite the warmth from the fire and a thick wool blanket, I had been near unconscious. It may have been minutes or even hours. Who knows?! But as soon as my eyes had flown open, I knew I could not linger, and here I was now seeing all these cold and hungry faces. What had happened?

"Get a fire going," I said to the nearest young girl.

My dress was soaked and torn. Mud clung to what was left of the hem. I had to get to my room for dry clothes, and I would need to get additional blankets for all the help huddled around the kitchen. They were all shivering.

"I'll be right back," I said. "Get a fire built up. We need to get some warmth in here."

I had just started up the grand staircase to my room, but then – as if there hadn't been enough drama – the front door crashed open.

A frightening bunch of soldiers stomped in – with no by-your-leave, nor any sort of greeting. There may have been a dozen or more. They were big and carried guns. Each looked more miserable than the other. Close to collapsing from fright, I sat awkwardly on a lower step, pulled the blanket more closely around me. Staring at them in disbelief, I think I cared little for what was next.

Rivulets of water were streaming onto the floor from their sopping-wet uniforms. Within minutes, each soldier stood in a puddle of his own making.

"Well, at least close the door," I said in a voice close to yelling to be heard. The wind was howling and blowing in enough rain to further soak us all. Two of the soldiers pushed the door shut and latched it securely.

"Ma'am," said the spokesman. He took a few

steps closer as he removed his hat. "We tried to get comfortable in your barn, but it appears it's not going to last much longer. We'll be needing a place for the night." He hadn't realized that he had been yelling, to be heard over the storm. But with the close of the door, that competition had been shut out. He lowered his voice and started again. "We'll be needing a place," he said in a calmer tone.

Of course, I recognized him – or at least recognized his voice. Did he choose to not acknowledge that he'd just saved my life and that of Dancy's not too many hours ago? He didn't ask after her or show any curiosity as to our well-being.

"Well, what's happened to the barn? Why can't you stay there?" I answered, waving my hand in the general direction of where it was located.

"Ma'am," he said. "There may have been a barn out there earlier, but there's not all that much left of it." As if to emphasize his point, a terrible crack made the whole house tremble and the windows rattle. He jumped ever so slightly, and I yelped in fear.

In two strides he was at the bottom of the stairs. His fingers reached out and rested on my arm. "It's a tree, Ma'am, no cause for alarm." He turned back to the men. "Corporal, go take a look."

"Yes sir," came the reply. He clung to the door but it slammed open. A fresh blast of rain splattered all of us. He hadn't stepped two feet out onto the porch when the wind slammed it shut again.

Hands pulled it back open. "It was a tree, Sir, lying on the front walk." He had stepped back in and three of the soldiers were wrestling with the door to push it closed.

Good grief I thought, those trees were huge. They'd surrounded and protected the house since forever keeping out the heat of the day with their dark shadows. I could not imagine anything having enough force to topple them. "Must've just missed us," said the soldier with his hand still on my arm. I pulled away.

"Please excuse me," he said, a sheepish look clouding his face. It was awkward. We eyed each other for a moment. His hand was extended, "I'm Lieutenant Ethan Hopkins, Ma'am with what's left of the 27th Regiment, South Carolina Infantry.

He looked down and realized he was dripping with rain. "Oh, sorry," he said, withdrawing his hand. "Is the Mistress of the house about?"

There was no doubt I looked like the bedraggled young child of some plantation owner. At least though I no longer wore my hair in braids. I had wound it in a tight coif this morning, but that was long gone. Having lost my bonnet, my once neat and tidy bun had let loose, and hair and curls were scattered everywhere, dripping like soaked trees after a summer rainstorm. My dress clung to me in a most inappropriate manner, and I had lost my shoes. I pulled the blanket more closely around me.

The words to thank him for saving us stuck in my throat. Instead, all that would come out was "For the present time, I'm in charge of Mulberry Cove." The words brought on a sudden wave of homesickness. And why not? Here I was with a group of Confederate troops who probably wanted to do who knows what. I had a kitchen filled with slaves, I had no idea where the field hands had run off to, and the world was about to be blown to smithereens by a storm the likes of which I had never seen.

Another huge crash from the outside. "Ma'am," said the one in charge, "It's a hurricane. Never seen one quite like this before. We've had a few over the past years, but best as

I can remember, never this severe." He cleared his throat. "Is anyone else about?" he asked.

"The slaves are in the kitchen," I answered.

His face darkened. "And how are they being treated?" he asked.

Why had I said that? His grey uniform said he was from the South. "Well," I answered, "You're from the south. Are you not a slaver? Isn't this what all the fighting is about?"

He eyed me and looked as though he had something to say but instead told the men behind him to "Search the house."

"How dare you," I began.

"It's orders Ma'am. Who knows who you might be hiding?" He scowled as he turned away from me. Was he expecting the entire Yankee Army to be hiding in the bedrooms?

A handful of soldiers pounded up the stairs – in search of what?

I mumbled something under my breath, wrapped my blanket closer, and walked back to the kitchen. They were all girls as best I could tell, and all were huddled together by the fireplace. They must have been hungry and were probably freezing. As hot as August was in the South, there was a chill brought on by the rain.

"You're going to need a larger fire," I said to

no one in particular and went into the pantry to see about food. I quickly realized I had no cooking experience whatsoever. I didn't know how to crack an egg or what went into a loaf of bread. I was at a complete loss when faced with bags of this and that and jugs and glass bottles filled with odd things. Searching the pantry, I hoped I'd recognize something.

Dried herbs hung in bunches spreading their scent through the air. It only made me even hungrier. I hadn't any idea what to do with the collection of foodstuffs. It was just a relief to see that there was something to eat.

Drawing myself up to my full height trying to look as though I knew what I was doing I said, "Surely someone knows how to prepare all this food." As the words came out of my mouth there stood the Lieutenant giving me yet another scowl as if to say what a twit I was.

His eyes traveled ever so slowly around the kitchen, taking in all the huddled bodies. Well, what did he expect? He was from the south, he knew about slaves. Not of my doing but nevertheless, they're here. Then to be sure to let me know just what he thought of the entire scene, he said something like "Can't you do anything for yourself? Were you that pampered wherever you came from that you don't even know your way around a kitchen?" His words were an angry whisper meant for my ears only. How dare he? A slow burn crept up my neck spreading its heat across my face. My response was just as cutting: "Do you?" I asked, "know your way around a kitchen? Perhaps this is an opportunity to help."

He turned on his heel and returned to the hall. Who did this man think he was? And in my home yet! Well, maybe not quite mine, but the only home I knew for now.

In minutes, two of the girls had built up a crackling fire in the hearth and another who looked closer to my age had gotten into the pantry and was bringing out sacks and crocks and jars of unknown contents and setting them on the table. By the look of the pans and bowls that they were setting out, I was sure they knew what they were doing. They spoke among themselves and appeared to have great confidence in all that they were putting together.

"Thank you," I said. They nodded, and I think I saw a few smiles.

Returning to the hall, I had to walk past those eyes that were boring into me. I wanted to stamp my foot and explain how I didn't belong here and the reasons for why I was here! But the words wouldn't come.

The soldiers were scattered about the floor, some with haversacks under their heads, some with the deep even breathing of an exhausted sleep.

"Lieutenant," said one of the soldiers, "All we found was a Negro sleeping on the couch. The house is clear."

The Lieutenant nodded. His blue eyes flashed a warning.

I answered the unasked question. "Indeed. It's Dancy and I'm on my way to check on her."

"Is she the one that we brought here earlier?" asked the Lieutenant. It was more of an accusation than a concern for her welfare.

"She fell into the river if it's any of your business." I pulled the blanket closer. It was very damp and provided little warmth. I stomped down the hall to the library to check on her. I didn't care if I woke up his entire Army.

All was quiet in the big room; Dancy was sleeping peacefully. I pulled the quilt up to her chin. I'd need to find one of my dresses for her to get her out of the sopping shift she was wearing.

The Lieutenant was at the door. "Ma'am, you do know the war is nearly over?" His voice wasn't loud, but the accusation was direct and clear.

"Indeed," I answered. "I was not aware of that, but here we are. And will you be releasing all of your captive people when you lose?" I certainly should not have said that and wondered where I found the audacity to speak up to a military officer. Perhaps they would tie me to a tree and shoot me!

"You are no doubt aware that not everyone in the South owns slaves." He followed me into the hall and would not leave me be. "Before this war, I was busy in my family's export business. We lived in Charleston. That's here in South Carolina. And for your information, we did not own slaves but had workers in our factory."

"Well I certainly know where Charleston is." Did he honestly think I did not know the whereabouts of some of their cities? I was baffled by his supposition of my ignorance. "Why are you here?" I asked. And then not waiting for an answer. "I want you out of my house," I added, coming up just short of stamping my foot. "Now."

"You're one of those Brit's aren't you?" he asked or rather told me, looking a bit more closely than was necessary.

"Indeed," I shot back.

"Well, after all the troubles in your land, you'd think you people would know about holding others in bondage."

"What do you know about my country?" I nearly spat, this time stamping my foot. I was so angry.

"Well, I know you practically starved the Irish to death twenty or so years ago and you would have if it hadn't been for the Americans coming to their aid."

"The Irish nearly starving to death has nothing to do with me or with slavery." It did and I knew it, but I wasn't going to give this uppity American the advantage. But he wouldn't stop.

"Seems to me you all were withholding food and with the taxes and landholders, the Irish people were being held in a type of bondage too."

And while he was busy insulting me, he was petting my dog. And my dog was as happy as could be, wagging his tail as if he'd found a new best friend!

But, that was the last straw. Now he'd done it. That was the end of my good manners. My instinct was to scratch his eyes out or just plain out spit. I'd never done that before! But I'd never been pushed to quite this point, and I knew it would feel really good to do it.

Instead, I stomped my foot so hard I thought my ankle was broken for sure. At the same moment, another huge tree came crashing down. A window shattered. I could hear the tinkling glass. It was probably coming from my bedroom. Gathering up my skirts, heavy from the soaking rain, I ran up the stairs. He was right behind me. "Don't you dare follow me!" I all but spat at him.

"You may need help."

"Certainly not your kind of help." It took moments only to get to my bedroom. Slamming the door behind me felt wonderful. For good measure, I threw the bolt. It was going to take some doing to stop fuming but, in the meantime, the wind was howling through the broken window bringing in sheets of rain. I could stuff the drapes into the gaping hole for a temporary cure and clean up the glass myself. Returning down the main staircase to find help would not be possible. I could, however, slip down the morning stairs, where I wouldn't be noticed, and try to get Dancy into dry clothes.

~

By morning they were gone. Lieutenant whatever his name was departed early, taking his troops with him. There was little to remind us that they'd all been camped out in the front hall. A few damp spots still remained, but they had taken all their haversacks, and it appeared that they'd mopped up the great puddles of the day before.

So hard to imagine after yesterday's destruction that it was now so sunny and bright and still. The air was clear and sparkling and for the moment none of the heavy humidity that crept into every nook and cranny on a summer's day. Had there really been a hurricane, if that's what they called it in this untamed and barbaric country?

Stepping out to the porch was like stepping into an unknown world. I could recognize almost nothing. Two of the magnolias had been blown over. Clods of dirt clung to their tangled roots. These were huge trees. So big, would we ever be able to cut them up to remove them? The trees that remained had so many limbs torn off that they looked like giant dark skeletons reaching up to the heavens. There was debris as far as the eye could see. The view was unrecognizable. Could such destruction ever be set to rights?

Only yesterday the barn had been hidden from the house by the thick grove of ancient trees. Now there was nothing between the main house and the barn. It was easy enough to see that the roof had been ripped off and one side nearly destroyed.

Shantytown was down the hill and couldn't be seen through what remained of the low-growing shrubs, but I could see parts of Mulberry Creek. It was no longer a creek but was furiously tumbling along the riverbed. Entire trees were being carried down the river, their roots a tangled mass.

What was making such a difference I wondered? Not only were so many of the trees broken and nearly leafless but the sun was warming the porch and the front of the house. Had that ever happened before? A home that had always been shrouded in darkness, where there had barely been a ray of sun and now the strong beams, cleared of all interference were brightening the entire area.

Sunlight was bathing the porch floor. It felt warm and enveloping like being wrapped in a fluffy feather-filled protective quilt. The light was so intense, the pillars were steaming from where they'd been soaked just yesterday.

Why couldn't I just sit here forever, soak up the sunshine, and not be concerned with all the damage and destruction and problems that were sure to come? What else could possibly happen?

TWELVE . . .

Malachi was making his way up the path. He may have been coming from what was left of the barn. He was shaking his head from side to side and mumbling words that only he could understand. His progress was slow as he picked his way around and over the fallen debris.

"Malachi," I called, "Over here." I tried to make my way between and around the fallen trees and broken limbs that littered the path. The torn branches of a live oak lay between us and would take some very unladylike climbing to get any closer.

"Where've you been? I've been so worried."

"Tryin' to catch up with them field hands 'fore they all rush off. And now, don' know what to do," he said, his voice rising to be heard. His forehead was a mass of dark worry lines. "We gonna need the help."

"Well, where exactly did they all go?" I asked. It truly did look hopeless, but I needed this man on my side. Thoughts of England kept pushing their way into my mind. Do whatever you like, I thought, find the field hands or let them go. I just want to return to my country. Leave this dastardly and uncivilized land.

"Don't know how we's gonna do it," he said. "Never seen nuthin' like this." This conversation was pulling my spirits down even lower.

"Indeed," I answered. "But, Malachi, can't we do the work? Can't we clean it up and fix what's broken?"

"Miz, you got no slaves lef' to speak of. Fields be flooded bad. Most of the crop is gone. Barn ain't no good no more." He shook his head back and forth. "Couple of yer animals left – not sure if we'll ever find them others."

Nothing he said was helping, but still I kept thinking: How could we just sit and do nothing?

"Malachi, one thing at a time. What do you mean we have no slaves left?"

"You heard them soldiers. North or South, them slaves should be free. Well, they hears it too. Mos' gone by now."

My words didn't want to come, they just wanted to stay in a knot in the pit of my stomach and remain there forever. Speechless I was, and how do I understand speechless when it had never happened before? He paid no notice and continued:

"You gots me still and Dancy if she heal right and there's a couple of young girls hadn't left yet. Not sure of them others."

"But how will we harvest the cotton?"

"Don't gotta worry no more 'bout the cotton. It mostly be gone." My knees gave out from under me, and I plopped down on the oak branch that I'd been leaning against. It was coming to me ever so slowly – no cotton, no money, no way to get back home.

"Well, what now?" I asked. I swiped at a tear, pretending to be pushing hair out of my eyes.

"Them soldiers s'posed to burn the place down."

"What?" I asked. "What are you talking about?"

"Heard 'em talkin'. S'posed to burn everything so's the Yanks don't get it – but they'da had no place to hole up in the hurr'cane if they'da burned the place down. You was spared, thanks to that storm."

Malachi had no more answers and all I had were questions. I watched as he hobbled back down the path.

"I want to go home," I whispered to the wind. It was all I could think. I want to go back to my own country. This isn't my home. I want to go back to the rolling green fields. Back to where they speak an English that is soft and precise and clearly understood. Back to the warmth of a country hearth with the peat moss throwing a warm heat and meals of fresh salmon and fresh-dug buttery potatoes.

But there was no home waiting for me. And how could I ever get back? There is no money for passage, and if I do get back what will I do? Where will I live? My school had indicated a desire to offer me a position when I had completed my studies, but I had left before I'd finished the last months of my education. Had I been fooling myself thinking I could return to the land of my birth? No one there wanted me. The headmistress had made it perfectly clear that my new life was to be in the United States of America.

How had I gotten to this godless wilderness of strange people with strange ideas and their odd way of distorting the King's English? I sat on the porch stairs and looked at the devastation around me. Over and over, all I could think was I wanted to leave. How was I going to do it? Where would I go? The warmth of the sun finally seeped into my bones. For a moment, it took the chill off.

I swiped at the tears that slipped down and were dripping onto the front of my dress. Somehow, someway, I was going to have to try to understand that there was no other place to go. Whatever was to become of me would happen here on this godforsaken piece of land. Here was where I was going to have to stay. This was not what I wanted, but here I was, and here I was probably going to starve to death.

"It will right itself tomorrow," Mum would say to me so often when all seemed bleak. I was so young then, but I had never forgotten her words. They went round and round in my head.

Here I sat, alone, at a place that was in shambles. I tried to see through the tears at what surrounded me. The house was going to need repairs. The yard may never be properly cleaned and brought back to what it had been.

So much to do. There was the big house with a few broken windows, some shutters hanging by one hinge and others dangling, splintered by the wind. When swept up, the paint chips on the porch floor would probably fill a mattress.

Every tree, as far as the eye could see, had been shorn of most of its leaves and many of its branches. Splintered trunks poked up everywhere like dark fingers reaching for the sun.

The barn, if it could be saved, had no roof. I could see the fields that just yesterday had been thick with intense white bolls of cotton as far as the eye could see. Today the fields looked like ghostly muddy quagmires with dead branches sticking out in all directions. Mud-spattered tufts of the once snowy-white cotton drooped on spindly plants.

I saw none of the slaves. Was I now really alone? Freedom sat on his haunches next to me, he nuzzled my ear and licked at my tears.

The sun was shining down and nearly blinding in its intensity. When was the last time this porch had seen the warm rays of the sun I wondered? The trees had kept the house in a constant deep and enveloping shade, keeping it cool during the hot summer months but also in dark shadows through most of the year. Now, with many of those ancient trees and branches lying on the ground, the sun streamed down on the house. The light was shining through. I moved down the walk, looking back. The house was sparkling as the sun reflected off the lingering raindrops.

What was it that I wanted? This had been the concern of Sister Teresa as I left my school in England. She said something like "You need to decide what it is you are in search of or what you desire from this life." My feet dragged, going in no particular direction.

And then, "Got lunch for you, Mistress. We miss breakfas'." That was more than Dancy had said to me in one encounter during the entire time I'd been here.

"Coming," I said, looking a little more closely at her. Her face had somehow changed – maybe not so tight around the mouth, maybe a softening in her eyes. Whatever had changed, she looked younger and prettier.

I sat at the grand mahogany table alone. Each time my fork touched the porcelain plate, an echo traveled through the room. I could stand it no longer. I picked up my plate and headed for the kitchen. Dancy rose quickly from the table as if I'd caught her doing something she shouldn't be doing.

"Sit," I said. She peeked at me from beneath hooded lids. "Sit," I said again, and this time pointed to the chair. "Now Dancy, I'm going to have to learn a few things quickly. Let's start by your telling me who is still here."

She was unable to answer the question. Just like that, she became a deaf-mute. I wondered why there was no answer, but I was hungrier than I could ever remember. I continued to shovel in pieces of cornbread and ham left from last night's dinner. My manners had just plain gone right out the window "Well, we do have some food. Why don't you eat, too?"

She looked puzzled, but I sensed that she was as hungry as I was. She took a piece of cornbread.

"Oh, for heaven's sake Dancy, eat some of that ham, too. Now listen to me: You are going to have to help me. As far as I know, there's no one else, and if there is, you're going to have to tell me who it is. We're here, both of us, and the only way that we're going to survive is if we work together."

"Yes'm," she answered.

"Now start with who is still here?" Hesitant, she spoke just a few names, some of which I'd never heard before.

"Have the rest run away?"

"Yes'm," she answered.

"I'm not sure where we're going to start in all of this," I said, "but there is at least some good news: We still have a roof over our heads."

Perhaps the reality of the situation had started to creep in. This was where I was going to be and be here for perhaps a very long time. I had nowhere else to go.

"Start wif' get the cotton in," she said.

"But there is none, Malachi said."

"Malachi blind as an ol' bat," she said while wiping at a spill on the kitchen table. "There still be some. 'Nuf to bring in."

Well now, another surprisingly lengthy response!

"Indeed," I said. 'You'll have to show me." I took a last bite of ham. I wondered if that was going to be the last meal that we'd have for a while. Pushing back my bench, I rose and went out the door. Dancy whispered an almost unintelligible "thank you."

I turned and wanted to ask – "thank you for what?" – but instead asked, "Have you ever been taught to read?" The side-to-side shake of her head was barely perceptible.

"How about if we give that a try in the evenings? I know so little of how to do things here, but I can read!" A slow smile that I'd never seen before crept up on her.

"Yes'm, that'd be fine."

~

The excess moisture in the fields was now draining back into the creek. It appeared that not all the cotton had been uprooted. There were still a few plants left with a few white bolls speckled with dots of mud. They stuck out like baby angels in a dark pit of tar.

This was wonderful, or so I thought. I still had no idea how one went about picking cotton. I'd worked some with planting it and then watched how they picked off the bugs and weeded it, but I knew nothing of harvesting.

"Malachi," I yelled. This was not the gentle voice of one who had attended one of the finest boarding schools in all of Great Britain. But I wasn't in England anymore, and at this moment boarding school seemed far in the past.

"Malachi," I yelled again, "Where the devil are you?" Oh my! I thought, with some embarrassment, isn't that just a surprising change from the gently reared young lady of not so long ago!

He appeared on the path, leaning heavily on his cane.

"Time for us to get to work," I said. His eyebrows shot up and he seemed to come to attention.

And we did: We got to work.

It took a few days for the plants to dry in the sun. And, of course, Malachi thought I was daft to try to harvest what was left, but there were no other options. He was patient in showing me how to pull a boll of cotton off the plant without getting the needle-like points of the tips stuck in my fingers. In one afternoon, I had nearly filled a sack from the crowns that had not been drowned in the floodwaters. My pricked fingers left only a few drops of blood on the snowy bolls.

"First time de' Mulberry ever risen that high," said Malachi. "Never seen the like. 'Course never seen a storm like that neither. Worse I ever seen." He scratched at his old head and squinted up – his eyes hoping to see the fields.

"Malachi, how about if I leave the bolls that are mud-soaked. maybe the next rainstorm will clean them and then the sun will dry them."

"Could," he said. "Won't be much worth savin'."

"Well, why?"

"Too dirty, too hard to clean."

"Well, we can't just leave it to rot in the sun. Tell me how to clean it."

And he did. It was laborious and tiring but

there was no other way. I had to wonder if we would even be able to salvage enough to get us through the coming months. How were we to survive? And then that same old question — to do what?

THIRTEEN . . .

Dancy, was not well enough to help. Her swollen ankle caused an awkward limp. And if possible, she was thinner, making her dark eyes even larger, giving her a soft doe-like look. Getting a meal together and keeping order to the house was close to impossible. And, as she informed me with hands firmly planted on her hips, she was not a field slave. "Never was, and never will be," she added. She did do her best to keep up with everything, but the house was too large for one young girl to tend to.

We were going to need more help. After my first afternoon, as the one in charge of what had once been a thriving cotton plantation, I knew it would take much more than just me to keep things going.

Shantytown was my destination. There was little left. Few shacks remained, and most of them were near falling down. I pushed open one of the doors, afraid it would come off in my hand. Two girls were cowering inside. Cowering from what? I wondered. I wasn't sure if I'd even seen them before.

"Would you like to work?" I asked. They looked at me with dark, frightened eyes. "Tell me your names."

One answered, "Hannah" and the other said "Flossy." "And what is the baby's name?" I asked.

"Calls him Baby," the younger one answered.

"Why that's not a name," I said. "Who does he belong to?"

"Belonged to old Janie."

"Where is she?" I asked.

"Died when he was borned."

Could this be true? And how many other things didn't I know about? And how do these things happen?

"Well come on, you can help in the fields. Bring him too, we'll at least be able to keep an eye on him." He was quite handsome with large dark inquisitive eyes and a half-grin. I held him for just a moment and realized how little I knew about babies. He smiled up at me. I didn't want to put him down, but he was squirmy and wanted to be off on some adventure. I watched for a moment as he crawled off with great confidence, certain of whatever his mission was. I wondered for just a moment if that would be something that would ever be part of my life. Would I, or did I, ever have that confidence or determination?

Cotton, I was to learn quickly, needs to be dry when it is packed, or it will mold – not unlike most things. Only after I had filled three sacks did Malachi share this piece of information – which, of course, I would've known if I'd thought it out a bit. But how were we going to clean and dry what looked like a huge amount of puffy soft white, or almost white, balls – or bolls, as they were called. Malachi said spread it in the sun. And where exactly would I be doing that?

Why the porch, of course. It ran the length of the front of the house. It was still mostly intact after the storm and was big enough to spread out what we had gathered. There was also the second-floor porch, which was even more open. The afternoon storms, although not quite as severe as the mid-summer storms, still happened often enough, but we could certainly keep an eye out for their approach.

The sun streamed onto the length of the porch for most of the day. It hadn't always been like this. But now, after so many of the magnolia branches had been broken in the storm or entire trees toppled, the sun nearly baked the front of the house during the day. With help from the others, we soon had fluffy tufts of cotton spread from one end of the porch to the other. The sun did its magic and dried those white cloud puffs as fast as we could pick them.

~

We had been working for so long and with little rest. And then, without even a "by-your-leave" or a knock, he stood there in the door-way. It gave Dancy the fright of her life. She'd been sweeping the long hall, singing in her warbly, thin voice. Most everyone smiled when they heard her, but no one could recall knowing any of her tunes. She made them up. And she never sang the same one twice. She'd create one after another, having more fun than anyone. But that day, she screeched.

He stood there – a makeshift crutch under one arm – the good arm. The other arm wasn't there; more accurately, from the elbow on down, it wasn't there.

Dancy thought it was a ghost. He was death-ly white except for the scraggly mouse-brown beard streaked with grey. It matched his hair exactly, making it hard to tell where one ended and the other began. There was a patch over what should have been an eye. It only half covered the angry red dent that ran from his forehead to his jaw.

Dancy stood back, cowering against the wall. She said later she wasn't sure who it was – he'd changed that much. But it was him, she was sure of it.

Burke Chamberlin. He was my uncle – or, better explained, my late Aunt Jane's husband; my family had no natural connection to this man. He had married my aunt years ago, after sending all the way to England for her.

And now, here he stood. Dancy had to run to find me, not sure what to do next. As I came to greet him, I saw the retreating back of a hunched-over driver as he rode off in a horse-drawn cart. Looking at the uncle, I wanted to chase after the wagon to ask questions. Questions like where had he come from, what had happened? But the wagon was already too far in the distance.

Curtsying, I said, "Welcome home, Uncle Burke." A blank look like a shadow passed over his face. Of course, I thought. How would he know who I was?

"It is a pleasure to meet you," I said. "Dancy, please bring tea into the library." That was the first time I had said that since leaving England! It felt so good, almost like expressing some hope of becoming part of a real civilization now that the owner had returned home.

He refused my offer to take his arm but limped along, dragging a shoeless foot that had merely a thick bandage wound round it. No boot. And this foot did not match the other. It was a few inches shorter.

Leaning heavily on his crutch, Uncle followed close behind, the thumping of his crutch echoing the length of the hall. I had the distinct impression that he was unsure of where he was going. After opening the library door, I tried to guide him in by taking his arm. Again, he pulled away, refusing any assistance.

"Please Sir, sit. We'll have tea in a moment." He said nothing but sat in the leather chair closest to the fireplace. "It is a pleasure to see you again, Uncle," I said. "We met years ago when you came to England to settle the estate of my parents."

I said the words but could remember little of how that had all taken place. I had been so young and could only remember how grief-stricken I had been. The little I remembered was that a very tall American who had appeared in our parlor had a booming voice and gave commands to anyone who was nearby. And then, not more than two days after his arrival, he had me tucked into a large coach where I was under the care of a tall and silent woman who frowned a lot. I recollect only that we went on a very long journey, and I was sorely tired. Our journey ended at a school where I was to live for well over a decade.

Dancy appeared at the door and said, "Tea, Mistress." How had she known to say even that much? Words had never come easily to her, try as I might to engage her in conversation. Our reading lessons may have been paying off.

"Thank you. Uncle, may I pour?" He again gave me a blank and unknowing stare from the eye that was not covered by the black patch. He looks like a bandit, I thought. I was not being unkind; I was just baffled as to what to do next. This was, after all, not my home. It was his.

The tea, weak as it was, was poured and, without permission, I dropped one very precious sugar cube into his cup. We had carefully rationed whatever we had, as there was so little.

He took no notice.

Again, I tried. "Uncle, do you not remember my mother? She was the sister of your wife? You had met her and my father before they died – do you not remember them?"

Not meaning to become exasperated, I tried again. "Uncle, what may I do to assist you?" And again, the blank stare. How were we to manage I thought.

When I rang the bell, Dancy appeared much more quickly than she ever had before. "Would you bring Malachi up to us, please Dancy?" She nodded, sensing that something was amiss.

Attempting to make polite conversation, I chattered on about the weather and the little I knew of crops. Thankfully I didn't have to chatter nonsensically for too long before Malachi appeared at the door.

"Ah, Malachi, please come in. I wonder if you could speak with Uncle Burke and determine what we could do to make him more comfortable." Malachi squinted a bit, trying to focus on his old owner. There was a flicker of recognition, but nothing more.

"I'll be out in the hall if you need me," I said, excusing myself.

What else could I have done? My thought

was: Perhaps Uncle would speak with his old friend and perhaps it was uncomfortable finding a stranger – me – in his home.

It wasn't more than an hour when Malachi emerged. He shook his head back and forth. "He gone," he said.

I gasped, "What do you mean?"

"His mind," he said, "It ain't there no more. He confused. He know some things but he's most gone."

"Does he know he's back in his own home?" I asked. "Back at Mulberry Cove?"

"Partly, but he not sure where he be. He do know me, but he not sure why."

"Dreadful," my voice came close to a whisper. "Now what do we do? My thoughts were so loud that they tumbled out in breathless, uneven sentences: "This war, why does it go on? Does anyone come back intact? Good grief! Do they know what they're doing, killing each other?" I couldn't seem to stop. "They're destroying everything they've worked so hard to create." My voice held a sob.

How could I cure this? How could I stop the madness of man's inhumanity to man? There had been such a loss of life and surely there would be more. I wanted to sit and cry. Cry for what could have been. Cry because I wanted to go home – and get as far away from this madness as possible.

And to think: It was less than one hundred years ago when these Americans had fought so long and so hard – all to create their own country and have independence. Independence from us, the British. And now look what they were doing. If it didn't stop soon, there'd be nothing left.

I swiped at a lone tear, determined that would be the only one. I was done with crying and besides, who cared?

"Malachi, could you stay here in the house with him?"

"Yes'm," he answered, then added almost in a whisper, "Had a manservant who went off to war with him. No tellin' where he's gotten off to."

"Well, so be it," I said.

The owner has returned. But this wasn't going to be a cure, I was sure of that. No doubt it was going to create even more problems. Problems I wanted nothing to do with.

FOURTEEN . . .

It hadn't been more than a week since the uncle's return! And there it was – a knock on the door. Dancy hastened to answer it, scurrying more quickly than was her usual style.

"Why Mr. Billingsley." There he stood hat in hand, just inside the hallway. "Thank you, Dancy," I said. He looked over at her and nodded.

"I must apologize," he began. "It took considerably longer than I expected to get here, what with all the fallen trees and branches and blocked roads."

"I had no idea you were coming," I answered, "But we've done our best to get some of it cleaned up." And I truly had no idea what could have brought him all the way out here. "But" I continued while trying to be the gracious hostess – I don't think we'd ever had a visitor. "I suspect it's going to be many months before we're able to get to much of it." I'm sure I looked a bit puzzled as I continued with a bit of polite conversation.

Trying to keep a pleasant tone and not sound too inquisitive, I asked, "And what brings you all this way?"

"You didn't send for me?" he asked, a curious look passed over his tired but questioning eyes.

"Why no. How could I? I haven't been to town in quite some time."

"Ahhhh," he said, as though a sudden truth was coming through. He glanced at Dancy, who was silently backing down the hall.

"I see," I said, not sure quite why she would do that. "Well, then, here you are." Lowering my voice, I added, "She has become oddly protective of me since the hurricane."

He nodded and smiled and said something about choosing to ride his horse rather than depend on a carriage or boat, as he wasn't sure of the urgency of the request.

"Your uncle has arrived home?" he asked. It was more of a statement than a question.

Still baffled as to his answering Dancy's request, I said, "Of course, that must be it. I'd forgotten that you knew him." Maybe I thought, I would have a friend in all of this.

"Please come this way," I said. "My uncle is in the library."

He nodded, no doubt realizing that this was why Dancy had requested he come. I had long assumed that no one else, other than the slaves that he kept, had been acquainted with my uncle. There were no neighbors that I knew of, and our brief and infrequent trips to town hadn't included meeting others. So, Mr. Billingsley was the only person I knew in all of America, which made me long for my home even more.

"Uncle," I said with a voice as cheery as I was able to muster. "Here is Mr. Billingsley come to call."

Mr. Billingsley stepped out from behind me and extended his hand. "How are you, Burke? It's been a while, hasn't it?" Uncle had been sitting forward leaning on his cane and, as if he were deaf and blind, ignored the greeting and the outstretched hand.

"I'll be just outside," I said, "If you should need anything." I excused myself, closing the door silently behind me.

It was nearly an hour later when Mr. Billingsley emerged. I rose from the hall bench to meet him. He did not look pleased. "If you have a few moments, please, could we chat?"

"Yes, of course," I answered, "And please, stay for dinner. I'm sure we have more than enough."

"Very kind of you," he answered, "then we'll have a chance to chat a bit."

"Excuse me a moment, I'll alert Dancy."

When I returned, we stood speaking in hushed tones, but not for very long. We had just a moment to touch on the hurricane, the price of cotton, and whether or not the river would be navigable anytime soon. There was no need to whisper, but we did so as if we were a couple of conspirators. In a very short time, Dancy came out to announce that dinner was served.

My guest and I sat across from each other, neither wanting to sit in the chair at the head of the table. Dancy had tried to get Uncle Burke to join us, but he would have none of it. He would not budge from what was becoming his favorite seat in the library. She brought a tray in to him, reporting back that he barely touched anything. But, she added, that was not unusual. Since his return he ate so little, she said, that it was a wonder he was able to stay alive. As usual, I asked myself "What could I do?" I was becoming accustomed to being nearly helpless with most problems.

"But, let me speak," said Mr. Billingsley. I had said nothing but nodded in his direction. He laid his fork down and began. "When chatting with your uncle, he had very little to say, but I tried to get some of the blanks filled in so's we could understand a little of what's gone on." He picked up his fork, but rather than eating much of anything, he used it to push the baked ham and collards around his plate to form some sort of odd pattern.

He then continued, "Your uncle has always been unusually proud of his deep roots in America. The graveyard that he kept down by the pecan trees was his pride and joy. Earlier in his life, he enjoyed pointing out one gravestone or another, telling the tale of this or that ancestor who had settled in South Carolina in the very earliest days of the colony."

He stopped for a moment and sighed. "And now it was his turn to fight for what he believed in. He was in Charlottesville where he was nearly blown to smithereens when he was leading a charge against the Yanks. But" he said, "that was back a ways. He was in a field hospital and then moved on to a hospital in Richmond." He stopped playing with his food and took a bite of his biscuit – a delicacy that Dancy was an expert at creating – so tasty that it didn't even need butter or a dousing of gravy. They were that good. There was a surprised look on Mr. Billingsley's face. He hadn't expected such a treat from a farm kitchen out in the wilderness. "Mmmmm," he said, obviously surprised by the delicious treat.

"Dancy," I said, without being asked. "She's the reason I haven't starved to death, but too, since the upheaval of the hurricane, she's become a friend." Maybe my only friend, I thought. "I've been teaching her to read. She's an excellent student."

Mr. Billingsley cleared his throat, then continued, solemnly, "You do know that teaching reading to the enslaved is prohibited here in the South." I gave him a blank look. "Teaching slaves to read," he added. I didn't know that but didn't want to show my ignorance.

"I'd keep a bit quiet about it if you want my opinion. And Dancy certainly knows the rules."

"But" he continued, "your uncle!" He brushed at the biscuit crumbs that had collected in his beard. "He's not sure who you are or why you're here. That's not so bad," he said. "But he does keep asking for Jane. I've tried to explain what's happened, but he's not wanting to know about it."

He was speaking between mouthfuls. There hadn't been more than a half dozen biscuits in the basket, but all were now gone. I was tempted to slide mine over to his plate to keep him talking. I'm sure he knew far more than I'd ever know. But instead, I interrupted.

"Mr. Billingsley, you are more than welcome to spend the night with us. The sun will be setting soon, and it would be treacherous finding your way back to town."

"Well thank you, my dear," he answered. "I will accept with pleasure." We finished soon after, leaving little on our plates. Food was still dear and would be for months to come, I was sure. Little was wasted or tossed to the chickens. By now, our discussion had fallen off to the price of cotton and the damage from the storm.

"Perhaps you'd care for a glass of claret in the library," I offered.

"Splendid," he answered. "We no doubt will be able to continue chatting, as your uncle seems to care little about what goes on around him."

The library was warm – too warm. No matter how many shawls we threw over Uncle's shoulders and lap, he always appeared chilled. Malachi kept a small fire in the hearth through most of the day, which seemed to satisfy Uncle.

Mr. Billingsley and I settled near the window, which offered a bit of coolness. He continued chatting about crops and how we could best get our cotton going again and where the best market was.

His suggestion was, of course, to go overland when trying to get it shipped out because there was still a blockade in Charleston. Such a trip would have to be undertaken very carefully, however, as there were troops everywhere and with a load of cotton, it would be best to trust no one – neither the Confederates nor the Yankees. He also said he could possibly pay a few bribes and get it out of either Charleston or up North of Wilmington on a ship, but it would take some time to get a plan together.

We'd been chatting quietly, one eye always watching for Uncle, but he hadn't moved or appeared to have heard anything we had said. And then Mr. Billingsley shared the revelation – one I had never even imagined.

"Your Aunt Jane," he began. His voice was lowered so only I could hear. "The aunt who you met," he took a sip of his claret. "The one who died." Yes, yes, I wanted to say, I knew exactly who he was talking about, of course. Why did he feel a need to clarify?

"Well, there's a story that needs to be told." He eyed his empty glass. I rose and refilled it, careful not to let it overflow the rim. I placed the glass in his hand and returned to my seat. I wasn't sure if I wanted him to continue.

"Hear me out," he said. He was hesitant. "You're not old enough yet to understand this, although you've had more than your share of upheavals. Life, as you may be learning, is rarely what we expected. There are shifts and upheavals all along the way." He paused for a moment as though collecting his thoughts.

"The new 'Aunt Jane,' was not a kind person. I'll cut right to the chase here." He sighed. "She had little regard for the slaves or their welfare. Her method of dealing with them was both cruel and inhumane. Therefore, there was quite a loss. Many ran away. And" he added, "a few didn't make it." I may have gasped, but words wouldn't come.

He had more to say, I was sure, but that was when Uncle started coughing in a manner that needed attention. He couldn't catch his breath. It was frightening. Mr. Billingsley tried to help. I rang for Dancy and asked her to find Malachi. He'd know what to do.

FIFTEEN . . .

In the morning we met for breakfast. Mr. Billingsley looked the devil, I'll say that much. Probably hadn't slept a wink and was undoubtedly anxious to return to the civilization of town. But I had to know more.

"Mr. Billingsley, please finish what you had started to tell me last evening. That Aunt Jane wasn't my aunt at all?" Perhaps, I thought, we could avoid any conversation about her peculiarities or cruelties to those employed by her, or better – those she owned. But I already had my suspicions.

Our meeting had ended so abruptly. Mr. Billingsley had started to address the "Aunt Jane" issue, but while chatting the uncle had gotten into his coughing fit. He needed all the attention that three of us could give him. Dancy had run back and forth for water, then rum, then a warm poultice to put on his chest. Once Malachi arrived, he and Mr. Billingsley were able to get Uncle up the stairs and into bed.

Now, this morning it felt awkward sitting at the massive mahogany table. At the head was the owner of this vast plantation. He cleared his throat now and again, but his coughing fit seemed to be over. I had almost no knowledge of this man. He ate little but clanked his fork often, perhaps to let us know he was still here. Hunched over and grizzled, he seemed unable to join the conversation, although we continued to direct questions to him. Perhaps he was totally deaf. I wasn't sure.

Mr. Billingsley and I chatted, our voices just above a whisper while enjoying our breakfast of grits and cornbread and what was left of the raspberry jam. He did relate how, after he had settled Uncle, he had gone in twice more during the night to try to calm him. Uncle's coughing was done, but night terrors then came over him. Malachi hadn't been able to settle him.

I no doubt had a blank look as Mr. Billingsley went to some effort to explain night terrors — that they were often a result of being in battle. Many soldiers relive the horrors of war in their minds for months or even years. For Uncle, whatever he was seeing in his head, may or may not ever leave. But, with some effort, one could sit and try to quiet him when he yelled about seeing things that no other eye could see.

"Your aunt," he began, then hesitated before continuing, "Your Aunt Jane came to this country on a ship, which you know. She was young. Old enough to be married, of course, but still very young to be traveling by herself."

Taking a sip of water, he looked at me over the top of his glass, "Young, much like you. And, if I might mention, there's a very strong resemblance." He closed his eyes for a moment. "The same almost blonde hair, very blue eyes, and the almost smile that she so often had." He cleared his throat before continuing. "The likeness was probably why I was so taken with you when we met on your passage to America."

"But," I said, "I met her before she died. I saw no resemblance."

"Yes, of course, and I'll get to that. But when she and I crossed the Atlantic, we found much in common and we very quickly became friends. By the time we arrived in Charleston, we didn't want to part, but she was promised." He let out a great sigh. Did his sigh indicate a reluctance to continue or maybe he was having a memory of what might have been?

"Your Uncle Burke," he nodded at the old

man sitting at the head of the table, "met the ship. They were betrothed. It was through an agreement that had been drawn up a year earlier when Burke had business in England. They barely knew each other. Your grandfather felt it would be advantageous to everyone and so allowed it. He felt that Jane would have far more opportunities in this country."

Pausing for a moment, he sipped at his very weak tea, now cooled to room temperature. He had presented us with a small package of tea that had probably been smuggled in from China. The only polite thing to do was share it, much as I wanted to tuck it away for only the most special occasions.

He continued. "I do believe your grandfather liked and trusted Burke and thought he'd give his eldest daughter a good life in America. She was your Mum's older sister, correct?"

"Yes," I answered, "there were just the two sisters."

Uncle Burke let out a snort type of sound, but he didn't appear to be understanding or hearing anything that we were discussing. Still, we kept our conversation just above a murmur.

"The wedding between your Uncle Burke and your Aunt Jane took place within the week of our arrival, so they could get back out to Mulberry Cove. The ceremony was done quietly, and few people attended."

He wiped at the grits that had fallen onto his lap. "They had a son within a few months of their marriage." A great sigh escaped. "Every now and then, I would see your aunt when she shopped in town." And then he added, "James, their son, died, which I had mentioned before. He died far earlier than he should have, and I felt responsible as I was accompanying him on the crossing to England where he was to attend school. It truly was a difficult time."

He broke apart another piece of cornbread and took some time smearing the last bit of sweet preserves on the gritty inside. I was determined to be patient.

And then he began again and seemed to brighten up just a bit. "When I met you aboard ship, I was returning to America after taking care of some business and visiting our, or rather her son's gravesite." Perhaps I gasped but wasn't sure. He quickly added "their son's gravesite."

Wiping at the trail of crumbs on the front of his wrinkled shirt, he continued, "You truly have a remarkable resemblance to your aunt."

Odd, I thought. I had seen no resemblance

at all – and I surely hoped there was none.

"But then," he sighed, "I did not return immediately, as I had further business in England and other parts of Europe. And then, as circumstances would have it, your Aunt Jane died before I could visit with her. I truly wanted to chat with her, maybe to calm her after the unfortunate circumstances of the son's death."

That time he did not say "her, their, or our" when referring to the son. There had to be so much more to this. What was he saying? When did Jane die? Was that not my aunt who we'd buried so soon after I arrived? I found myself unable to speak.

"Now, the part that I'm sure you aren't aware of." He seemed reluctant to continue, but cleared his throat, looked over at Uncle, and continued "I was in Europe when she died. She died of the yellow fever. Unfortunately." I was becoming increasingly confused. I was here when Aunt Jane died!

He continued. "My trip was prolonged due to business and while I was away, not only had your aunt died, but Burke had remarried." He cleared his throat and sipped at the bit of warmish water still in his cup.

"For whatever reason, they called her Jane.

I'm quite sure that was not her real name. She took what little was left of your inheritance and spent it however she wanted. It was the trust that had been left to you in your real Aunt Jane's care." I'm sure I gasped at least once.

He looked a bit sheepish but continued. "No one was really aware of what had happened, as the country was in turmoil and Burke was doing his best to keep up with the demands of a large plantation. The people in town were so busy just trying to understand what was going on between the North and the South that they didn't much care what neighboring individuals were doing with their lives."

Was the shock obvious? Did he see that I had no idea at all of any of this? I must have gasped yet again, as even Uncle Burke, for just a moment, seemed to raise an eyebrow. What I'd just heard had to be the explanation: she hadn't been the Jane that I'd met, and who had died soon after I arrived, and had no resemblance to what I remember of my family and she had shown no interest in me. So then, I wondered, what remained of my inheritance? Was it all gone? Had she squandered everything? Could that be why the money no longer arrived to pay for my education? Of course!

Mr. Billingsley was quite obviously upset by this meeting. He would eye Uncle Burke now and again, but there wasn't even a flicker of recognition from Uncle as he continued to clank his fork as he pushed his eggs and biscuits around his plate.

And that was the end of it. Mr. Billingsley rose abruptly and took his leave.

What was I to do with this new information? How was I to continue? It felt as if the door had been closed on my ever returning home – home to England, away from this barbaric and uncivilized country. I was sure of one thing – and one thing only: I did not belong here!

SIXTEEN . . .

It was time to plant. That's what Malachi said, "Get them seeds in now," were his words. "Soil has warmed some and maybe it gonna do better this year." He said this as his rheumy old eyes searched the landscape. But where was the seed?

"Not sure just how well it's gonna do," he said as he scratched his unshaven chin. "Hasn't been none too good for the past few years. Last year's flood an' all sure don' help none."

"What do you mean?" I asked, "Why hasn't it been good?"

"Soil's just plain tuckered out," he answered. "Happens some with cotton. There's no stoppin' it – soil gets plain ol' tired. Crop come in much heavier when I was a young buck."

"Why is that?" I asked, not quite sure what he was talking about.

"Well, you can jus' pull so much good out of the soil, then there jus' t'aint nothin' more and plants get scraaaaaaawwny like bunches of old scarecrows."

"But you had said that you spread the animal manure on the fields in the fall."

"Do some," was his quick answer. "But" he continued, "Hard to replace all that's been drunk up by them cotton bolls."

"Back in England, they planted different crops, which kept that from happening," I said, rather proud of my answer, considering how little I knew about agriculture. My school had been self-sufficient when it came to food. Surrounding the main buildings were fields that were farmed, but we students had little to do with them.

We had, however, learned just a bit about the "starving time" in Ireland. It had an impact on our country but was rarely discussed or even mentioned. What I did learn in class was that if the Irish had switched crops from one year to the next, it could well have been the answer to keeping the soil healthy.

"What you sayin'?" Malachi asked.

"The school," I said, "my school in England had a very large garden. We raised all of our own food and I know they grew different crops each year." I wasn't sure how much further to go, but continued; "A terrible famine had spread through Ireland. Many people died from starvation. Potatoes were their main crop and then the blight came. They were indeed in very serious trouble."

I took a deep breath. This wasn't a pleasant topic for either the Irish or the English. But at school, they taught us a bit about planting. At least, we came away knowing a cabbage from a potato.

It was difficult to understand just who was in charge of Mulberry Cove. Maybe they once had this information, but apparently, it had been lost long ago.

"Hmm," he said. "Used to do somethin' like that. How you know this?" he asked, his eyes squinted up with suspicion.

"I know this much," I responded but didn't add that, most assuredly, this was not my favorite course in school: "A farmer needs to change his crop now and again. There were tales told that the Irish had always done that, but then they put that routine aside and would plant the same potatoes in the same plots, year after year. All the goodness that was needed to grow potatoes was taken out of the soil, and there was nothing left."

I was actually enjoying it a bit – sharing the little I remembered. "The potato was vulnerable, and the blight came. After losing so much, the Irish went back to the old ways; and, once again, put in different crops each year. One year potatoes were planted and the next year peas or some such. They would simply switch fields."

I stopped; I had paid little attention in that class. In truth, I absorbed not much more than a lecture, a brief pause we took from studying endless European history and learning the proper manners when serving tea. But I did remember that the sadness and devastation that Ireland experienced must have been overwhelming, whether the Brits wanted to talk about it or not.

"They called it the 'starving time'," I added, "for good reason."

I'm sure that was more than Malachi ever wanted to know. His feet were doing a little tap dance, not wanting to be still another minute.

"Wait just a moment, I'll fetch my bonnet." My enthusiasm was sorely lagging, but I stayed close on his heels as I followed him down to the fields.

The workers were busy pushing the seeds into the soft dark reddish soil. Even the youngest children were busy doing their part. This was going to be my job, too, if we were to ever get it all in. The tilled rows went as far as I could see.

"Workin' for weeks," said Malachi, knowing I was staring in awe at the fields ready and waiting for the seed. "Not much help left, but a few change they minds and return. We's doin' what we can."

"I can do this too," I thought to myself.

"Yup," said Malachi, "You sure can." It took me a moment to realize that I'd said it out loud."We talk later 'bout yer rotatin'."

"Well then, show me what to do."

And there it started.

I became a cotton farmer. Most assuredly not what I wanted or ever dreamed I'd be doing, but pushing the seed into the soft soil was not all that difficult – at first. As the day wore on, coming close to noon, with the sun high overhead, it became increasingly more difficult to bend to get that seed planted. When Dancy brought our noon meal, I thought I wouldn't be able to make it to the side of the field. Everything hurt.

Mumbling an excuse, I left and limped toward the path that wound its way up to the house.

How, I wondered, can they do this, day after tedious day? The weather for now still had a bit of spring coolness. But how does this get done in the terrible heat that engulfs and suffocates the land during the summer months? Putting one tired foot in front of the other, I made slow progress on my way back to the house. Malachi appeared out of nowhere, a talent he seemed to have perfected.

"Doin' o.k.?" he asked. I was sure I saw a hint of a smile.

"A bit worn perhaps," I answered. "But, Malachi, here's a question: Have there been fields that haven't been planted in cotton in a while?"

"Yup, surely are." He answered. "Some been lyin' fallow down on the so' side that we haven't got to since the war got it's beginnin'."

"Well then, I know they're trying to get the farmers planting food crops, tell me what would do well there. Potatoes maybe?" I truly missed our nearly steady feast of potatoes served so often and in so many ways. They didn't seem to be important here in America's South. Dancy had pulled a few from her kitchen garden, but for whatever reason, potatoes were not one of their favorites.

"Can a'ways plant peas," he answered. So, he wasn't fond of potatoes either. "Then there's collards and there's corn. Had a few acres where the corn was growin' 'til last year's harvest. 'Course there's sweet potatoes, but not yer favorite." I thought I caught a bit of a twinkle in his clouded eyes.

"Why not put some of the cottonseeds where the corn was and move the corn to another field. And, if it would keep everyone happy, why not more space for your favorite sweet potatoes?" Goodness, I thought, I'm standing here planning my crops like a common farmer!

"Miz, you talkin' like we's got enough negras to farm the state o' So' Carolina," he said, wagging his head back and forth. "We gonna have trouble gettin' this field in."

"We'll try," I answered. "We'll do what we can."

Was this to be my new role? It was going to be hard not to get discouraged listening to his words of hopelessness, but I was willing to do as much as possible. Anything, I thought, is better than watching these acres and acres of land lie fallow and become weed-infested. There is so much here – and so little.

I did not want to return to the field of

backbreaking work. Maybe they wouldn't notice if I took some time off. All my sore bones said it would be best to disappear for a while, and maybe even curl up with one of the hundreds of books that filled the library shelves. Who read all those books I wondered.

Everything hurt, but how could I give up so easily? There'll be a chance to read some other day.

Aching bones and all, I returned to one of the plowed fields. It was late afternoon. The slaves had slowed but hadn't stopped. Tired as they must have been, I was sure I heard them singing. I wondered: How do they do that, after their endless day? I dug the toe of my boot into the soft reddish soil and thought – maybe not as regretfully as I should have – was this to be my life?

SEVENTEEN . . .

The sun was lower in the sky. Dark shadows were cast by the skeleton trees. There would still be a few hours of daylight, but aching bones said there was nothing more I could do, I had done enough for today.

Freedom had been napping in the shade and bounded over the ridges of newly mounded dirt as I put one tired foot in front of the other. He was a friend to everyone. – Well, Uncle Burke anyhow, and, of course, me. He gave the slaves a wide berth. They had little interest in befriending an animal. Malachi had once mumbled something about the four-legged creatures eating better than the two-legged ones.

Rubbing at the small of my back, trying to pretend it really wasn't hurting that badly, I watched as my shaggy friend trotted through the field, sniffing each new mound of dirt. I took off my boots. I'd carry them. I knew better then to be barefoot, but I think I had blisters on top of blisters.

And there, not a foot away, was a woodchuck. Freedom yipped in delight. The woodchuck no doubt saw him first, as it was already scrambling, with its rolling run, towards the woods. This was fair game. He had a chance at least with a woodchuck, never a deer; although he didn't know that and still raced off in hot pursuit, whenever he had the chance. In a flick of exuberance, he scurried off, barking in a grand chase.

He didn't return. I'd have to chase after him, but I'd need my boots, and I was not going to put them back on 'til I'd soaked these feet in a tub of very warm soapy water. I was giving him little attention; I only knew that his barking became fainter. I'll need to go find him was a thought. He can't be far, but first I'll find a cold drink and wash my face and eat a bit of cheese and bread. We'd be in the nighttime darkness soon enough. The slaves were still busy, although it was easy enough to see that the pace had slowed.

I stood for a moment to admire the row upon row that had been worked today. Malachi gave a wave and then made his way over from the group. I could tell he wanted to chat. "Goin' fine so far," he said.

"It does seem to be working. There's so much to do but the people all seem to know what's required. Thank you for your help, Malachi. They listen to you."We stood for just a moment watching the activity and listening to the soft sounds of songs shared within the group — the words not really meant to be understood.

Then, I saw it.

"Malachi," I screeched. It looked like nothing more than a twig between the rows. He saw it too, how I can't imagine with his sight so clouded. But there it was. It slithered over the mounds of dirt.

I froze. It was inches from my foot, my bare-foot. I had my boots, but I was carrying them, not wearing them. I knew better, but there it was, ready to strike. Malachi grabbed my arm and yanked me out of the way. He was in front of me and quick as a flash he stomped on it, with boots held together by rawhide strips. There were more holes than leather.

The snake wasn't very big. And it struck. It was a copperhead, which I was to find out later. I knew nothing of snakes. In an instant, it struck its target — the exposed skin below Mala-chi's worn cotton trousers and the top of his ragged old boot. Malachi yelped. He knew what it was.

With eyes nearly blinded by thick cloudy film, he reached down to grab the curling, slithering serpent, but he couldn't see. The snake then sank its teeth into his outstretched hand.

I screamed for help. Three of the workers heard and raced across the field, leaping over the furrowed rows. I tried to catch Malachi as his knees buckled. His eyes were wide open. They had a questioning look.

"Help him!" I yelled between sobs. I had no idea what to do. "Bring him to the house. Hurry."

It seemed to take forever.

"Where's Dancy, for heaven's sake?" I said to no one in particular as we slammed the door open. The field hands were carrying him as gently as possible. And then there she was. We stretched Malachi out on the couch in the library and pulled a blanket up to his chin.

"What do we do?" I asked over and over. I knew nothing of snakebite.

Dancy brought warm cloths to wrap around the puncture holes, but his hand and ankle had swollen to the size of melons. They turned a deep purple. He was slipping away, his breathing slowed, becoming shallow. He didn't move.

My tears wouldn't stop as I tried to hold one of the warm compresses to his badly discolored and swollen ankle. It was happening so fast.

"Malachi, don't leave us. This is my fault," I said over and over.

His eyes fluttered open, and for all the world, he looked as though he could see me as clearly as he'd ever seen anything. A half-smile played at the corners of his mouth.

"Damien," he said, although I wasn't sure if I'd heard him correctly.

His eyes bored into me. "Find him, you gotta have help," he said. "He be Massa's son." His voice was a whisper, but he said it as clearly as if he'd been standing tall next to me.

"What?" I said. Had I heard him correctly? Dancy was leaning over him and I'm sure she was doing more than wiping off perspiration when she held the damp rag across his lips. And then she gave an ever-so-slight nod.

"Hush, now," she said and moved the cloth back to cooling his forehead.

His eyes closed and his chest rose one more time. Then came a long exhale. His body relaxed as if covered in peace.

Dancy sat on the couch cradling his head on her lap as tears dripped down, falling on his sunken cheeks.

This can't be, I thought over and over. Tears would not stop. Dancy pulled the blanket up over Malachi's face, covering his staring eyes. What had he said? Surely, I hadn't heard him correctly, but then Dancy had given an ever-so-slight nod. My only thought was: How would I manage without him? This couldn't be!

Tears flowed as my thoughts went back to England: There, I reminded myself, we didn't have snakes, or hurricanes, or sweltering heat, or soldiers who gave you no peace, or slaves who worked the land.

"I want to go home," I cried softly, not meaning to be heard. I miss my hills and green fields and civilized people who enjoy tea and walks in the park and quiet conversations.

The grief I felt might have been not only for Malachi, but for the turn my life had taken. My apron was soaked, as there was no embroidered handkerchief to catch the tears.

I wanted to yell. I wanted to hit someone, I wanted to shake Malachi awake. Instead – I left the room. I had to clear my head. Closing the door with more force than necessary, I went off in search of Freedom. Where was he? I needed him, now more than ever. I had no friends. I had no family. Where could I go to hide and to get away from all this?

Walking out into the falling darkness, I thought I'll just breathe the air and try to be calm. I went to the edge of the woods. The sun that was slowly sinking into the western sky lit up the path as though it were high noon. With so many trees blown down from the storm, it was easy enough to see I was going through what had once been a very thick grove of tangled trees. There was a hush and a quiet and a closeness not felt out in the fields or even up by the house. I called Freedom's name a few times, but there was no answer. I really should have been frightened by the long shadows and being alone as dark was quickly descending. But it was a peaceful sort of quiet, maybe just what I needed at the moment as my tears slowed and then stopped.

I called Freedom again and again, but there was nothing. Following what may have been a deer path I walked until it was too dark to see where it would lead. The path ended abruptly in a meadow. How long had I been walking? I wondered. Feeling the sadness and regrets of the day overtaking my good sense, I sat for just a moment at the bottom of a gnarled old oak. It was time to return. To get back to whatever awaited me. The sun had set a while ago. A misty moonlight filtered through the canopy of green, giving just enough light. I needed to get back. But, which way?

I set off, stumbling for much of the time. My feet were more tired than could be imagined. How long had I walked? It could have been hours. The moon was nearly covered by dark clouds. There was little light. For just a moment I sat in the shelter of a massive bent-over oak, its branches drooping to the ground.

It must have been the whoo-whooing of the owl that woke me. Where was I? The darkness was thick and menacing. What had I done and how had I gotten here and how would I ever find my way back? My cotton dress gave little warmth. It must have been very late. What foolishness had I gotten myself into now? I called Freedom again, knowing the ridiculousness of ever finding him this late.

The chill of the night was seeping into my bones. I was alone. Then, a twig snapped. Footsteps? I couldn't move, frozen where I was. Perhaps it had been a deer? The dark offered no clue.

I barely breathed, frightened into stillness. I wanted to call out again to Freedom but hardly dared to even take a breath. Perhaps it had been an animal. Weariness overtook me. I put my head on folded arms and bit back tears. I needed to think, to come up with a plan. Tiredness won out, and I slipped into a troubled and restless sleep.

A hand reached out from behind me. I had been paralyzed from sleep and couldn't remember where I was or why. I was so cold. Dark fingers closed around my wrist.

"Don't turn," said a low husky voice. I knew that voice, but kept my head down, letting my hair fall where it may. I dared not move as a cloth was tied around my mouth, like a muzzle, silencing me. A rope was tied around my wrists. It too was taut. It would not be easy to slip out of. My voice would not come. The gag had silenced me. "Yer a far piece from home," said the voice. It was a gravelly whisper. "Yer never gonna find yer way back." The hush of the voice was caught in the wind. "If you try to run yer jus' gonna git yerself more lost."

"Git you to a road," he said, in little more than a whisper, giving me a push. This couldn't be happening. How and who had found me?

I walked, pushed along from behind and gagged by the cloth. "Don't turn 'round," said the voice. Then, "watch yo'self" as we stepped over fallen branches. It was so dark. Wherever we were, it was a trail along a gurgling gentle stream. He seemed familiar with the path, pushing me forward. We walked and we walked, and it was not easy. After what may have been hours, when I was near falling down, as well as close to starving, I tried to ask where we were going. The gag stopped my words.

Then the voice, in a raspy whisper, said, "Here. Stay here and wait. Someone be comin'. Sit." A hand pushed me down onto a log. "Don' try to follow and don' turn 'round." I dared not look, but listened to his rapidly retreating footsteps. Footsteps that were uneven. Was he limping?

What now? My hands were bound at the wrist. There was no way to remove the gag that silenced me. But I knew that voice.

It must have been close to morning. There was a chill in the air and my world was becoming darker. Tiredness overtook me. And then I heard them. Hard to tell who they were, but they spoke in the heavy accent of the South. They were shuffling through the underbrush, through the long dark shadows. I wasn't sure if I'd been left in the middle of a road or where I was. The ropes binding my wrists seemed to get tighter as I fumbled to free my hands. Who was coming? Was it the Yankees or the Confederates, and what would I say? Shouldn't I be hiding? I did nothing except tremble and try to hold back the tears that were springing forth from fright or anger. I wasn't sure which.

"Oh, lookie what we have here." The voice came from not too far away.

"'Pears to be a damsel in some sort of distress."

I dared not move. There was no way to speak or to observe who it was shuffling towards me.

They chatted among themselves – four or five of them, it seemed.

"Dis be about the bes' thing we's come upon in months," said one of the voices.

"What'da ya think we should do with her? And what's she doin' here?

Then a loud young voice said, "I'm thinkin' someone mighta left her right here for us to find."

"Yer crazy, Sarge. There's no such."

"Then why'd they tie her up?"

They were so close I could smell their stinking foul breath. They were bent over me. A hand grabbed my arm in a grip that I thought would break it in two.

"C'mon," said the voice of what may have been the sergeant. "We'll take her with us." Two arms and hands lifted me to standing. My trembling only got worse.

"Move," said the one holding my arm. "We got ourselves a mighty fine treat here."

My legs had turned to water, and I tripped. The hand holding my arm jerked me back up, but my legs failed me again. I fell into a heap on the ground. I could not rise. I had no strength left. The hand gripping my arm yanked me up and threw me over his shoulder like a sack of meal. He hadn't bothered to untie my hands or to remove the gag that was stopping my words.

"Over there," said a gruff voice. "Best we stay out of sight 'til this all settles. Take the trail into them woods." He slapped me on my rear. "It's all gonna be over in another couple weeks, then we can return home like nuthin's happened."

"Tell 'em we was captured," said one of the gravely voices. "Tell 'em all we jus' got ourselves outta one of them prisons."

Raspy laughter followed. It was laughter with a mean edge.

"Oh drat." I could feel him tense. His hand moved away from where he had been rubbing my derriere.

"Oh my gawd! Run." It sounded like an order from the sergeant.

And he did. I bounced up and down on his shoulder.

I could hear the approaching horses, their hooves pounding the ground.

"Drop her. Run," yelled one of the pack. He did. I was just plain let go of to fall into brambles and dirt.

"You three, go after them," said a voice from someone astride an approaching horse.

Horses galloped past me. So close. Did they not see me? I scrambled to try to sit. Brambles tore at my arms. My skirt was caught and ripped in my struggle. I think I was screaming, but any noises were muffled by the cloth tied over my mouth.

A voice from high up on a horse said, "What have we here? My, it appears to be Miz Amelia." This couldn't be. "What an unexpected surprise. Here, let me." I knew that voice.The horse snorted and the saddle creaked as the rider dismounted. His voice sounded startled and surprised but then "G'wan ahead," he yelled to whoever else was traveling with him.

"Yes sir, Lieutenant," answered a voice, as a number of horses trotted away.

"Now, Miz Amelia, what in heaven's name are you doing here? It appears that you've gotten yourself in some sort of jam. May I help?" He was working with his knife to cut the gag that kept me silent. "Interesting," he mused.

That all too familiar voice. Why, of all the people in the world did it have to be him coming down this path at this moment?

Tears were welling up. "Get me out of this," I muttered, trying not to sound as if I was about to collapse in a wash of tears. In no time, he had both the fabric covering my mouth and the rope tying my wrists tossed aside.

"Well now," he said. "This can't be how a big plantation owner such as yourself spends most of her days?" There was a smile twitching at the corners of his mouth.

"I was kidnapped," I said, not very kindly. My voice was raspy.

"Kidnapped?" His eyebrows rose in disbelief. For just a moment, I took note of how tall and nice-looking he was. There was a very concerned look in his very blue eyes. "Well," he said, "that fella back there said we were needed up ahead."

"What fella?" I asked, surprising myself by using a word so common to an American. I rubbed my wrists, trying to get some feeling back. "I was lost."

A doubting look passed over his eyes.

"Whoever did this found me back in the forest. He didn't want me to know who he was." How could I answer the questioning look in his eyes? He probably didn't believe what I was saying. And I could not even answer my own questions: Where was I, ... and why? Trying to explain how I had been chasing after a dog just wasn't going to be believed.

"And then the others came along," I added. Tears forced an end to the telling. Was this to be my life forevermore?

EIGHTEEN . . .

Once again, I was lifted up onto the lieutenant's saddle. He rode with his arm tight around my waist. "Maybe you're ready to tell me the story of why you'd been captured by a group of renegade soldiers?"

"No," was my all-too-quick answer.

"Well now, that's not a very polite response to the man who just rescued you from who knows what harm that could have befallen you. You know, they have panthers and mountain lions and wolves here." His arm tightened. "Not to mention the group that was running off with you into the woods. You should be thanking me from the bottom of your little British heart." There was a smile in his voice.

After he cleared his throat, his voice became serious. "The renegades who were running off with you surely will be found and escorted back to camp, where they'll no doubt have a better reception. 'Pears they were deserters, which wouldn't go well if they were caught by either side. The war is over," he said, "And it's our plan to return home."

We heard that the war was ending, but was it really over? We were so far removed from town that rarely did we have any news. But now, perhaps, if it were true, I could return home – back to England.

"Met a fellow aways back," he said. "Told us this was the best road if we were heading back to camp." This was followed by a long "Hmmm, I wonder," he said. "Perhaps he knew who'd be here to greet us."

I wanted to ask if the fellow who'd suggested this way had a peg leg and long dark hair. But I already knew the answer.

And with that good news and the fact that he'd saved me from who-knows-what awful fate, it was difficult to maintain my haughty attitude toward this very cocky lieutenant. I chose to remain mute. He, however, felt the need to chatter the entire way. I must have been shivering despite the warmth of the day. He unbuttoned his coat and placed it around my shoulders. It felt oddly comforting.

"My home is in Charleston. Haven't been out this way more'n once, but we've been busy chasing those Yankee troops out of our home-land. Especially those that don't know the war's over." He said that last bit almost in a whisper. "But" he added on a lighter note, "I have been observing your cotton crops."

We were trotting along at a nice pace. Not the most comfortable situation I'd ever been in, but I was no longer lost in the woods or being held by a group of outlaw soldiers.

Whether I'd been listening or not, he didn't seem to care, and so continued: "My father has been an exporter of bales of your cotton for the past few years. He ships them to the factories up north," adding, "to be woven into cloth. A lucrative business, to be sure." We were going at a gentle rhythm and my eyes were closing but he continued. "I was in school in New Eng-land, and knew little about the business." I must have shown some interest as he contin-ued. "That is until this war got started. Very little cotton traveling north now. But you must know that."

The gentle trotting of the horse was threat-ening to lull me to sleep, but he now had my at-tention. Much as I did not want to be engaged in conversation with this man, I couldn't help asking, "Surely there's a way to get the cotton

North?" My voice was raspy from disuse.

"Why, how nice," he said, "She can speak." This remark was uncalled for, but what was I to do? Hop down and walk all the way home – which was, I assumed, where we were going. Never mind, I still had no idea where I was or which way to go.

"Not sure as a plantation owner why you don't know this, but there have been blockades in most of the harbors, preventing any transportation, other than troops, in or out." I was quite sure I knew as much or more than he did about blockades. It was, after all, a blockade runner that had carried me into this country. But that would remain a tale for another day.

"Actually," he continued, "Had to get a fellow named Billingsley out of here."

"Billingsley?" I said. Now he had my attention. "How on earth do you know that man?" I was reluctant to show too much interest. But I was quite sure he must have been acquainted with him when he seemed to stiffen.

"And what exactly is your connection to a scoundrel like Billingsley?" he asked.

"I met him on the ship."

"Hmm," he said.

"On the crossing," I added. I felt it wasn't

necessary to share any details about what ship we were on, or of Billingsley's connections to my aunt.

"Coming from England, no doubt," he said, then added a "Hmm," as if coming to a new understanding. "In any case, we caught up with him a few days ago and got him out of here," he said. "They were on to him."

"Who was on to him?" I asked. "I don't understand."

"Well, no doubt you knew he paid for the cotton that you had, small as the shipment was. Well, he was in Charleston, where he had it loaded to get it to a mill up North. They thought he was taking it to England. He loaded it on a ship bound for England. But then, being a long-time friend of the captain, he was able to have the ship diverted to New York before crossing the Atlantic with some other cargo. That's where they unloaded the cotton and got it to the mills up in New England. 'Course there are very few even in business up there anymore, thanks to the war."

"But Billingsley owns property here," I said, trying to understand how this all made sense.

"Yes, he does and made a sham of providing food to the Confederate troops. He has been known to work both sides of this war if you can understand what I'm saying." He paused for a moment. "Not only was he getting cotton to the North but he has in the past provided the North with some not very accurate information on where the Confederate troops were headed. So, rather than having him hung or putting him before a firing squad, they turned a blind eye to all his doings."

Oh my, I thought. So much I didn't know. His arm around my waist tightened. It kept me from falling off the horse. My heart was beating fast, and I was feeling a mite unsteady.

"He's done some good," he continued, "so we can't be too hard on him."

"But," I said, not sure if I wanted to engage this person in further conversation, "what are other planters doing with their cotton?"

"Not sure," he answered. "What they can't get shipped out I do believe some of them are burning." He couldn't miss my gasp. "They were trying to keep it out of the hands of the Yankees."

His next utterance was a foreboding "Uh oh."

Now what?! I wondered with exasperation. Was I to find no peace in this country? He yanked at the reins as he steered the horse into a thick copse of trees, signaling his men to follow. "Quiet," he whispered. "If you say a word, I'm going to have to gag you and tie you up and leave you here for the mountain lions."

Is this man insane? I thought. First, he saves me from kidnappers, and perhaps other terrors, then he wants to have me eaten by wild animals? But there was no time to reason it out. We were deep in the thick covering of trees and could just make out a large group of soldiers approaching. Most on horseback. Some walking. Why I thought, does he think I would ever give away our hiding place?

As the soldiers approached, they were bantering back and forth, apparently unconcerned about stealth. The giveaway was the blue uniforms, all tattered and shabby. It was a ragtag group of Yankee soldiers. I do believe I was shaking, but from fright or cold, I wasn't sure. The lieutenant's arm brought me closer. He whispered close to my ear, "The war is over, but not everyone cares, and there's still enough trouble out there to get another one going."

It seemed longer but probably took only a few minutes for all the Yanks to pass by. We waited a while in silence, longer than necessary, no doubt, to be certain there were no stragglers. My patience was coming to an end when I blurted out. "Exactly what quarrel do you think I have with the North?"

When I turned around to see him, the lieutenant's blank look told me he had no idea why I would ask such a question. Leave it for another day, I thought. All I wanted was to get back home. I wanted a bath. I wanted to wash my hair. I wanted a warm cup of tea, and I wanted to be left alone. I wasn't really concerned about an answer, and so be it, my question hung in the air unanswered.

"G'wan," he said, slapping the reins. The horse responded instantly, and we headed, in what I hoped, and somehow trusted, was the direction of my home. And there it was. I said it if only to myself. I was calling the plantation home. But, if truth be told, I had no other.

The sun was dropping in the late afternoon sky as the horse plodded up the drive to the front of the house. "Ha!" he said. "And look who's here to greet you."

Freedom was on the porch, barking and leaping about. I think I started to laugh a bit, watching his wild dance of excitement.

The lieutenant was also close to laughing at the dog's excited welcome. "Well then, that's a fine welcome. Isn't he the reason you wandered off?" he asked. Wandered off? It didn't need an answer. He dismounted, set me down on the ground, and straightened up, "It was a pleasure." A half-smile pulled at the corners of his mouth. And then, for a moment, he showed a puzzled look as the rocking motion at the end of the porch caught his eye. He raised an eyebrow, not masking his curiosity.

"My uncle," was all I said. There was too much to explain. I let it go.

He looked again, quizzically, at the gently rocking figure, then back to me, but said no more. He simply tipped his hat and returned to his horse.

"Well, thank you," I said, not completely forgetting my manners. For a moment I thought – maybe I didn't want him to go.

"And where is it you're off to?" I called to his retreating back.

"Catching up with my men. Heading back to Charleston." He turned and touched the brim of his hat as a farewell. "Perhaps we'll meet again."

With that, he slapped the reins and trotted off without so much as a backward glance.

NINETEEN . . .

It was over.

The cotton reaching for the warmth of the sun had pushed green sprouts through the dark soil. The newly emerged corn looked like a vast forest of thin leaves moving in delicate waves in the spring breeze. We had already been enjoying the fresh just-picked peas. And it was over. The war had come to an end.

Endless years of strife and death, and dying and sickness, and starvation and loneliness, and horror, and as simple as that – "It's over."

We've made it, I thought. How? I had no idea.

And really? That was when Damien had come up to the house. I was tying my bonnet, trying to make a bow instead of just a knot that would later have to be undone. The bonnet was threadbare and had ties that resembled thin strands of yarn rather than the wide grosgrain ribbon that had been the original colorful ties.

I met him on the porch.

"It's over," he said. Just like that. But I already knew. But why was he here? Dancy appeared out of nowhere and stood a moment. They eyed each other and looked like they had something to say. Dancy did a nervous shuffle with her feet, her lips wanting to form words, but then she turned and disappeared back into the house.

"Hmmm," I thought. But said only, "What is it, Damien?" I wasn't sure if I should fear this man or hug him. I knew he was the one who led me out of the woods when I was lost. But at that time, for whatever reason, he didn't want me to know it had been him.

"With the war over, I'll be needin' a job. Not much out there and looks like you could use the help what with Malachi gone." He shifted for a moment, favoring the peg that was the lower half of one leg.

What could I say? We needed every bit of help we could get. And, if Malachi's dying words were correct, it was just possible that the old man rocking in the chair at the end of the porch could be this man's father.

"Indeed," I said, "but there'll be no whips or other punishments. Do we understand each other?"

He nodded and for a moment I thought he looked contrite, which did not suit him well at all.

"Then you'll start immediately," I said. It was a question more than a statement.

"Of course."

"And there's the promise of no harsh punishments?" I said again.

I was just barely able to understand him, as he shook his head back and forth and mumbled, "These are my people. You think I enjoy hurtin' 'em?"

He turned to leave, but then turned back and walked towards the old man in the rocker. Uncle Burke was rocking gently back and forth, keeping time to some rhythm that only he could hear. Scrunchy noises came from under the rockers, as he continued the mindless movement, back and forth.

Damien reached a finger out and touched Uncle's gnarled hand, and, for just a moment, it looked as if Uncle showed a flicker of recognition. It was true then. I was sure of it. The facial features were indeed similar, especially the high cheekbones. They shared the same tall bony physique, with long fingers and massive muscular shoulders. Father and son. Indeed!

Damien turned abruptly and stomped off the porch, his peg leg thumping, accentuating his awkward gait. Dealing with his ways will take patience, but he knows more than anyone else on how to keep everything going.

Dancy noiselessly appeared and stood a few feet to the left of me. I had a feeling she'd been observing us from the window.

"Tell me this," I said to her, "Is he Burke's son?"

Her answer was a half nod and a mumbled "Big Bertha."

"Thank you, Dancy."

Damien was heading down the walk, but turned back once and nodded to Dancy. She smiled.

Uncle Burke had continued his rocking. He may have heard part of our conversation. But would he have understood? It was hard to tell.

I stood in front of him. "It's over. The war is over."

Did he care? Did he know what I'd said? I don't think so, although an eyebrow rose a bit, the one over the good eye. That was more facial expression than I'd seen since he arrived home. He was shriveling down to nothing. I was sure he wouldn't be with us for much longer. He refused to eat most anything we served and seemed to have given up or had crawled into that great dark hole in his mind that he no doubt called home. He showed little interest in his surroundings or what went on as he rocked back and forth.

I patted his hand and turned back to Dancy. I needed to go to town and resupply our larder with what was left of the few coins that Uncle had brought back with him.

"Dancy," I said, "come with me. We can take the wagon into town. I'm sure between the two of us we'll manage." She was reluctant but walked with me to the barn.

"We're going to have to ask for more credit no doubt. I have little left." Dancy nodded. She had become my friend. There was many a time when I would chat about something with her, and she would come up with the answer. She had been raised here. She knew most everything there was to know about this sprawling plantation.

"Well, der's always that silver," said Dancy.

I was tired. I didn't want to play games with her. She would sometimes go off on subjects I knew nothing about, but then I was sure she didn't want me to know just how some things got accomplished on this plantation. And no doubt I was better off not knowing the why and wherefore of everything.

"What silver is that?" I asked, expecting little further information.

"Why 'da silver that Miz Jane buried."

"What silver did she bury?" I asked. "And which Miz Jane?" But I had little interest in the ridiculousness of buried silver and whatever game Dancy was playing.

"Why Miz Jane buried 'da lot of it way long ago when she hear tell there might be a war comin' on."

"Which Miz Jane?" I asked again, but perhaps that didn't really matter. Dancy had my interest. I recalled having heard that the ladies in the South had gone and buried their treasures to keep them out of the hands of the invading Yankees.

"First one." She answered.

"Dancy, you need to tell me now: What are you talking about?"

"Well, Massa know 'bout it too." Her voice seemed to be picking up strength.

"Yes," I said, "but he doesn't seem to remember anything or even know where he is.

Now tell me what you're talking about."

"When Miz Jane get sick she worry someone gonna get that silver so she bury it out under the bench, out by the mulberry tree. Out by 'da summer kitchen."

"Dancy, are you sure? Why didn't you tell me this before?" I asked, my annoyance coming through.

"Don't recall you askin' me."

And that was the end of that conversation, but then she led me right to the spot she had described.

And there it was. Right where she said it would be.

"Dancy, how did you know?" But she stood back with a half-smile, knowing my delight.

The garden bench had been cumbersome and too heavy to be moved. So, I had knelt down and used a garden trowel, to begin digging beneath it. Whatever, if anything, that had been buried there had been there for quite some time because the grass covering it was growing in thick patches and there were tangled roots to dig through. It looked much like any other part of the garden, which would have kept it from being noticed. Dancy had gotten down to help me. It took us a while, and the hole was fairly deep when her trowel had struck the box.

"Aha!" she'd said – a look of amused, "I told you so" in her dark eyes.

More than anything, the box resembled a child's coffin. Heavy as it was, it took two of us to pull it out of the dark hole. It was filled with such treasure – dining silver, creamers, sugar bowls, small platters, candleholders, even four silver bracelets, and a brooch. This must have been what was originally in the house as there were so few pieces left in the dining room. It looked like a fortune worth of valuables. Together we picked up the box and headed for the kitchen.

"Now what to do?" I said out loud.

She gave a "Hmmm," and then pointed to the pantry. When we set the heavy box down, she marched off as if on a life-and-death mission. I heard the scraping as she moved the empty tins once loaded with tea, and the wooden crates, now empty of all the flour and cornmeal they once held. Dancy pulled them all off the shelves, stacking them on the floor. There was a small door in the wall. Sticking one finger in the hole where there once had been a doorknob, she pulled it open. It was dark and cool and empty. "There," she said, "It be safe." I looked at her, searching for an answer as to why there was a small closet tucked in the wall of the pantry. Her look told me there wasn't going to be an answer.

The box almost didn't fit, but we both gave it a good shove and it was in. We closed the door and Dancy stacked all the empty tins and crates back on the shelves. It covered our secret place.

I pushed the pair of candleholders I'd taken deep into my apron pocket. "Dancy," I said, "Come with me. We should go now. Let's get the wagon. I'm sure between the two of us we can manage."

And so off we went, thankful that I wasn't the one handling a pair of old mules. Dancy took the reins and did a fine job of guiding and directing. She was no longer a slave, thanks to emancipation, and she knew this fact better than I did. She had learned to read, easily I might add, and she was rather proud of her ability.

Life was so changed from anything she'd ever known. I had offered her a small wage if she'd stay on at Mulberry Cove. After all, she knew more about the property than most, including me. Readily agreeing, we had easily slipped into another relationship. No longer was she someone's property, but was now employed and was my friend – and dare I say, my only friend? Being employed suited her and she seemed to have more interest in what she was doing, and she was trying to help me with sewing. However, my awkwardness was nearly embarrassing. My only skill, I believe, was in monogramming tea towels with tiny embroidery stitches, and I rather doubted that the opportunity to do fine handwork would ever present itself again.

But today was a fine day, blessedly cool, without the summer's heavy heat. We chatted now and again, which Dancy almost seemed to be enjoying. We passed what looked like what may have once been fields. "And what is that, Dancy?" I asked. Or better, "They look like fields but too wet." It took only a moment for her to respond. "Rice fields," she said.

"Of course," I said, "Malachi had told me that long ago rice had been grown here." And then, more as a musing, I said, "I wonder if it can be done again?" Well, sure enough, Dancy heard me.

"Got a Gullah cousin," she said. "Down in the low country." Not sure how, but I remembered that Malachi had also said it was the Gullahs who had the knowledge required for growing rice. Very different from cotton farming he'd insisted. Was this possible? Could this be done?

"Hmmm!" I truly believed that both Dancy and I had the same thought.

As we entered the town, it was eerily quiet. A very elderly soldier, leaning on a makeshift and rickety crutch, was being guided by a young child. A lone dog walked by. He was also limping, much like the crippled soldier. It was like a ghost town. There was a hush like a great pause as if no one was quite sure if they should be celebrating or crying. The South had not been victorious, and although the people had been accepting of the war's outcome, they surely were not happy. The only life that the South knew was forever gone. There wasn't going to be a way to continue farming the huge cotton plantations without the slaves to help. No single farmer could ever handle the planting and growing of the huge crops that were traditionally grown here in the South. I knew this as well as anyone. They were all going to have to rethink how to continue, and it was going to be a long road to rebuild all that had been destroyed.

But then, what were the slaves to do? They owned no property. They had no jobs. Few were literate. Their families had often been split up, and they had nowhere to go. Very much like me, I thought, with no family, no skills, and no home to go to.

Life was changing again.

Dancy and I made our necessary purchases. Mr. Brown, the shopkeeper, had more than a pound of rice that he agreed to sell us. Maybe just maybe, what I believe was to be my new home, would be ready for rice to be reintroduced. Was it possible that in the grand scheme of things, this could once again become a prosperous plantation?

Our canvas bags were heavy as we secured them in the back of the wagon. We headed for home.

TWENTY . . .

We were in the beginning days of summer. The heat was creeping back in after the welcome coolness of the spring days. Other than the changing seasons, there was little difference in the day-to-day life between wartime and peacetime. Rarely had we even seen any soldiers or any of the terrible destruction that had gone on. We were back in the hinterlands, so our lives continued on with little interference. The work never stopped and seemed more tiring than ever. The cotton was in full flower, the peas had been harvested and the corn stalks were nearly as tall as I was. Dancy's small kitchen garden was thriving. She was rather proud that she had never been a field slave, but she certainly had a knack for growing things. Damien I'm sure had been there more than once to help and show her the way of a vegetable patch.

And now, here it was June. The day was promising with the warmth of the sunshine —

too early still for the afternoon thunderstorms that were part of the heavy heat of summer. I had run down to the field to inspect the corn. The ears, tucked in the long frond-like leaves, still had a ways to go.

The dreadful hurricane, that had changed so much of the landscape now seemed so long ago. Most all the debris and trees and branches had been chopped and stacked for firewood, but ghostly skeletons of formerly powerful trees remained – maybe so's we'd never forget?

I heard the clip-clop of hooves before I saw the rider approaching.

Now what I thought. I stepped behind the split trunk of what had once been a mighty oak. I was alone. All the workers were in the fields. We had been warned that there were still a few rogue soldiers wandering about and we should take care as they could be dangerous.

A rider sitting high on his mount, in no particular rush, clip-clopped up the long curved lane that led to the house.

Peeking from behind the tree I caught a glimpse of a horse that looked a mite worn. A tall rider sat astride, moving with the gentle rhythm of the clip-clopping pace. The leather saddle sent out a quiet creak with each step.

Whoever it was looked comfortable and in no particular rush. The sun was behind him. Goodness, he certainly looked regal sitting up there so tall. He didn't appear to be a threat although there was a long rifle tucked within easy reach at the side of the saddle.

He saw me peeking from behind the tree. He tipped his hat. "Hello," he said. And then, "Amelia, isn't it?" A wide smile spread across his face. He took a moment, then said, "Lieutenant Ethan Hopkins at your service." I'm sure I turned a bright red with embarrassment, having been caught hiding behind a tree. But there was a smile in his voice. "You're here alone no doubt." His eyes crinkled up as he smiled. "It's been a while, but you've been on my mind." He was flicking the reins in his hands, looking a bit unsure, but continued. "I know you're fully capable of handling all that this plantation has to offer, but you could no doubt use another pair of hands." I was sure he could see the questions that I wanted to blurt out. I twisted my hands around in my apron, words just wouldn't come.

He adjusted himself in the saddle and looked over at me with a smile that refused to be held back. "I've never worked the land, was trained in the business end of it, but I'm sure I could learn."

I came out from behind the tree and stared up at him. Of course. That unmistakable and distinctive deep southern accent – and that un-shakable confidence. It was him. Could this really be?

And why was I feeling such relief? Why was I grinning so foolishly up at him? I wasn't quite sure why and I wasn't sure what to say or do.

I blurted out "Lieutenant!"

He smiled. A wonderful smile that lit up his eyes.

"Yes, of course," I answered, "I could use the help." Words started to spill out. Words I had no control over. Why was I jabbering so much but I couldn't seem to stop? In fact, for no reason that I could think of a few tears slipped out.

I'm not sure why but quite suddenly I was telling him everything while using my apron to swipe at the escaping tears. I told him about Malachi and the snake and how he had saved me, and how things had not been the same without him, and that there was no one who could replace him. I told him how Uncle wasn't doing well and how we were going to try to grow rice and that we had help, but not enough. I guess I was telling him everything and the tears that had been dribbling, were flowing un-checked.

He had looked a bit baffled but then jumped down from the saddle. "I'm here," he said. His arms went around me in a most protective embrace. For a moment only his lips grazed my forehead. I shivered. It was a nice shiver. "I know just a bit about farming," he said, "and what I don't know I can learn." His eyes were so kind. "Just like you did," he said.

There was a hesitant smile. He cleared his throat. His eyes were taking in all of me. "Amelia," he said, and for a moment only, his words seemed to get stuck. He choked back what may have been more caring than he was prepared to show. "Somehow, you've been stuck in my head." One hand was rubbing my back. The other was touching my hair. "I knew I had to return."

It was hard not to smile through the tears, I used my apron to dry what was dripping from my chin. "And" he added, "You know that my family was involved in cotton in Charleston."

He held me at arm's length, eyeing me so closely and with such concern. He cleared his throat then continued. "I want to take care of you," he said. "Take care of you forever."

I think I hiccupped but then had to smile

through the tears. A protective arm slipped around my shoulders. I think I shivered. A nice shiver. Indeed, I couldn't remember when anyone had ever done that. It felt so good. I didn't want to move.

We stood there for who knows how long looking out over the land. The sun was just above the horizon. It was burning off the morning fog. Sparkling droplets of dew on the new shoots of green pushing up through the soil reflected the morning sunlight with the promise of a fine new day.

We could hear the workers departing Shantytown; their melodious voices drifted through the air. The words of their music meant only for themselves. They were off to spend their day cutting back the weeds, crushing the pests, and with hope and strength work to bring another crop to market. They needed a source of income as much as we did, and we needed the help.

Acres and acres sprawled before us. So much change. So much promise. Maybe there was more strength here than I knew. One I hadn't felt before. Oddly, I was sure that with the lieutenant by my side, we could change this and create a whole new way of living, bringing life and love and appreciation back to the land

and to the people. He wiped at the tears dripping from my chin with a corner of my already damp apron.

"I'm here," he said, "You won't be alone ever again."

Words wouldn't come, but the warmth of his arm was something that couldn't be imagined.

Looking out over the vastness spread before us, I knew this now: This was to be my home. It had been a long road, but now I was sure, this was where I belonged. Perhaps together we could do some good. Maybe create a new way of life – isn't that what they had all fought so hard for and had sacrificed so much for?

The land was here. The help was here – with a bit of guidance, endless hours, perseverance, and a bit of luck we could claim a job well done. Hadn't Malachi said life tosses the unexpected at us, and most times for the good? The rewards would come.

The lieutenant's arms were around me. It was a protective and caring embrace. Somehow, I knew that together we would move forward and somehow, someway create a better life for all.

POSTSCRIPT . . .

And that was what I was able to piece together that summer just before my senior year. With the bits of information that I could find I was able to recreate one girl's story. There was little to go by, except for the old green ledger and Amelia's notes, which were scattered and not in any particular order. Often, they appeared to be tear-stained, but she had a careful hand, although faded, most of what she had written could, with a bit of effort, be read.

There was no accounting as to what happened to the plantation. Why had it been neglected and discarded? Grandmom was reluctant to say much, which added to the mystery of why it had been abandoned and left to the vagaries of nature. Maybe that tale was going to be for another day.

The last entry in Amelia's journal was that she and Lieutenant Ethan Hopkins had married with Dancy and Damien in attendance. Beyond that the words were not legible. They had faded into obscurity.

FACTOIDS

- South Carolina was the first state to secede from the Union. Referred to as the Palmetto State, a likeness of the palmetto palm was added to the flag in 1861. Readmitted to the Union in 1868, the palmetto remained a symbol of South Carolina.

- On April 12, 1861, the Confederates fired on the Union troops at Fort Sumter, South Carolina. Thus began the Civil War. Four years later on April 9, 1865, Robert E. Lee surrendered to Ulysses S. Grant at the Appomattox Courthouse in Virginia, ending the War.

- Set up by Union forces, blockades along the southern coastal states halted much of the exportation of cotton to New England and European countries.

- Many blockade runners were successful in importing guns and munitions from England to the southern ports. If they were successful, they would then carry a load of cotton or other goods to the North or to Great Britain, where cotton was woven into fabric.

- Plantations were often left in financial ruin as the blockades curtailed much of the market for cotton. Many of the mills in the north also did not survive the Civil War due to the blockades which ended shipments out of the south.

- During the Civil War the Confederates had over 250,000 deaths. The Union lost over 350,000. Of those, diseases such as dysentery were by far the leading killer of troops.

- More than 1/4 of the white male population of South Carolina, who served in the military during the Civil War were killed. This accounted for more deaths than any other state in the nation.

- In the 18th and 19th centuries, many entrepreneurs in America tried to create the much-prized silk fabric. Most were not successful due to the intricacies, labor, and knowledge necessary to raise silkworms and weaving the fine threads from the cocoons into fabric. Mulberry trees, still seen throughout the South were the silkworm's source of food.

- Cotton was king throughout much of the South during the 1800s. Harvested by hand, it wasn't until the first half of the 20th century that mechanical devices were perfected to end the laborious task.

- Cotton was probably not native to America but was introduced from the Caribbean Islands and Mexico. It was cultivated in Florida in the mid-1500s and Jamestown, Virginia in the early 1600s.

- The introduction and cultivation of rice began in the lowlands of the Carolinas in the 1600s. A difficult and labor-intensive, but profitable crop, its success is attributed to the Gullahs, a group of Africans from areas in and around Sierra Leone in Africa.

- Hurricanes often impact the east coast of America. Although there were no major hurricanes in South Carolina during the Civil War, over 40 have been recorded since 1850, the most destructive of which took place in 1989, with recorded wind speeds in excess of 130 mph.

- South Carolina was the lead producer of rice until the late 1800s when destructive hurricanes destroyed much of the lowlands. By the end of the 19th-century, rice production in the Low Country had fallen to unprofitable levels, shifting the growing and cultivations to Louisiana, Arkansas, and Texas.

- Importation of the enslaved became illegal in 1808 throughout the United States, although South Carolina continued the practice. From the early 1800s, more than half the population of South Carolina were slaves. ~ The 13th amendment, created in 1865, abolished slavery. For economic purposes, some former slaves chose to stay on the plantations where they had been enslaved. Many died from disease and hunger.

- The Emancipation Proclamation issued by President Abraham Lincoln in 1862, freed more than 3,500,000 slaves. Many of the freed slaves then went on to fight with the Union Army. After the war some became landowners, others tenant farmers or sharecroppers, while others worked for wages.

Antietam
Waking the Fury

Emily at 15 is bored and annoyed with just about everything and everybody. Tired of her chores and irritated by the endless care of three younger sisters, she would like to have a life of her own. Her parents are absent; her Father is off fighting a war she doesn't understand and her Mother has left for Pennsylvania. As the eldest of the four sisters, she must take responsibility for her home and family. When the bloodiest battle of the Civil War is fought almost on her doorstep she is unwillingly pressed into service. Emily is called on to make decisions and to take charge of wounded soldiers while fending off the invading troops and protecting her younger sisters. Life changes forever as she discovers a courage that she did not know she possessed. Strengths emerge as she stands up for her beliefs while sheltering the enemy and caring for a runaway slave, both of which hold very serious consequences. In this remarkably accurate depiction of the Battle of Antietam, a legend is once more uncovered. It involves a mass of very angry bees. This dangerous, stinging swarm may well have had an influence on the outcome of that fateful day in 1862.

Jennie Wade
A Girl From Gettysburg

It had been foolish to stay but now there was no choice. It was anyone's guess what the outcome would be. Nothing was as it should be. Oddly, the Confederate troops were pouring in from the north and Union troops were marching in from the south. They arrived in droves. The town was not prepared for what happened during the early days of the summer, 1863. Jennie, a young local girl, did her best to keep up with the demand for bread and water and medical care for the troops. Her brothers were scattered, her sister would soon be having a baby, her mother was not bearing up well and Jack, her intended, had not been heard from in weeks. It was a time and place that would be recorded in American history forever. A time marked by the largest number of casualties in the Civil War. It was Gettysburg, Pennsylvania, a small, unremarkable town; an easily forgotten town that would live in infamy and one that history would never forget. Of the almost 50,000 casualties of that encounter in early July, only one civilian was killed. This is her story. The story of Jennie Wade, a dedicated young woman thrown into the middle of one of Americans' most tragic times.

Mists of the Blue Ridge

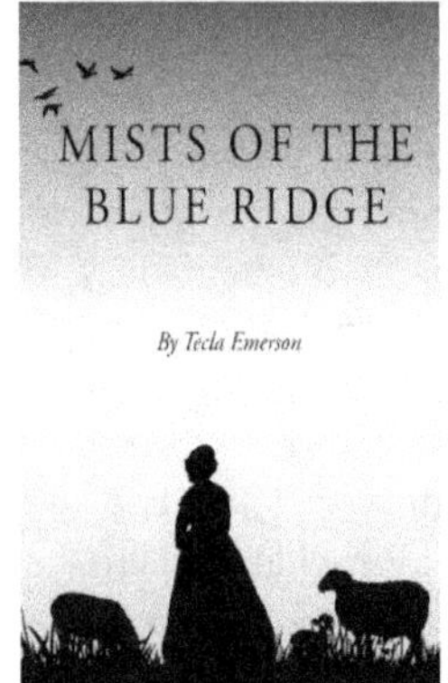

Olivia lived a quiet and protected life tucked away on a farm in the Blue Ridge Mountains. It was far from the great war that had been raging between the North and the South. She had little interest in the who and the why of it all, and wasn't even sure where her sympathies lay. Then, without warning, the conflict surrounded her. At 16, she was ill prepared for the responsibilities that were thrust on her.

This is her story. It's a tale that tells of courage, determination and survival during one of America's most trying times.

Hidden in the Early Light
a tale of the Irish famine

Katy was 16 when the hard times came.
Her father disappeared in the night and her
mother left her with a tiny baby sister. She
was suddenly thrust into the role of caretaker. It was a responsibility she didn't
want. The farming life was not for her and
now she had to find a way to survive and
to keep her younger brothers from starving. How could she ever be free of a life
she hadn't chosen?

It was the 1840s and thousands were dying from the great potato
famine, one of history's most dreadful events.

This is Katy's story, the story of how a young girl survived by using her wits, determination and courage.

Shadows in the Fog
A Block Island Tale

Milly lived on an island far away from the mainland. She was an orphan and there was no one to care for her. Sent to live in a house filled with boys she was pressed into the role of cook and caretaker. Her life became that of a servant.

When an unfortunate incident took place that threatened to scar her forever, she was sent to live with an angered and bitter veteran of the Civil War.

Living the life of a recluse and with battle scars of his own, he keeps his past hidden from all. Hidden until Milly comes to stay.

This is the tale of a young girl's quest for survival and how she brings herself out of the depths of despair as she learns of her mysterious past. Uplifting and compelling, the tale follows Milly as she matures and accepts all that life has given her.

Gift of the Winds
A Tale of Hendricks Head Lighthouse

In the late 1800s a ferocious nor'easter traveled up the New England coast. It forced a three-masted schooner up on the rocks. It was within sight of the Hendricks Head Lighthouse. History says there were no survivors. However, a trunk was found that had been washed ashore. It held a most unusual and interesting surprise.

The tale unfolds through Abigail's diary. It tells of the unfortunate event that condemned her to the life of a recluse in Ireland. Life is difficult for her, but determined to survive; an inner strength takes over. Alone, she sets out for a new life in America.

Andersonville:
The Long Journey Home

Hock snuck off in the dark of night to join the Union Army. He was too young to be part of the fighting force but now, taller than most, he easily joined their ranks.

Wounded in the battle at Petersburg he was captured and sent to a Confederate prisoner-of-war camp – a camp so horrid, it is still written of today. As one more of Andersonville's nameless inmates, he was given a number. Identified as "Unknown 9586," he was thrown on the death cart and hauled out as one of the dead. "Unknown 9586," did not rest in peace. Leaving the site of his burial, he set out for the north. Alone, starving, wounded and unarmed he began his journey. This is his story. From the hills of Vermont to the sights and scenes of horror that are found on battlefields and then to his final destination. It's the tale of prisoner #9586 – Unknown. The prisoner who missed his own burial.

Indentured Servant

"My being for ever banished from your sight?" Who was this "...undutiful and Disobedient Child" who in 1756 penned a letter to her father in England? What had she done to so offend him? Why, as a well educated young girl, had she become an indentured servant? Why was she alone? In her letter, she pleads with her father to forgive her and to at least send her a bit of clothing. "...almost naked, no shoes nor stockings to wear."

Here, within these pages, the mystery of Elizabeth Sprigs is revealed. It is a tale based on a single letter sent from Baltimore so long ago.

The Oregon Trail:
Pathway to the West

Maddie knew the trip wouldn't be easy. Her mother and older brother were no longer with them and Hannah, her little sister, was hers alone to care for. And Hannah was mute. Mute for reasons no one knew.

It would take months to arrive at their destination. Months that would include accidents, floods, Indian attacks and disease. The losses along the trail were both huge and unexpected. Would they ever reach the West, the land of their new home?

They traveled in covered wagons, on horseback and many times on foot. They risked all that they had, over the rough and not well-organized trails. It was a time filled with mystery and unknowns. There were few firsthand accounts of what lay before them and for some of the travelers the long trip would have disastrous results.

It was 1845. A small group of daring and brave pioneers set out with high hopes and all their worldly goods to head for a new life. A new life in what was soon to become the Oregon Territory.

www.ingramcontent.com/pod-product-compliance
Lightning Source LLC
Chambersburg PA
CBHW071432200726
48294CB00002B/606